HIDDEN

LEA CHERRY

For all those who need to feel like there is always hope.

CHAPTER 1

Eye of Newt, the local juice and coffee café, spilled over with customers awaiting their orders. Teenagers took up residency at the sidewalk tables, eager to discuss what they had planned for summer break. Umbrellas were open over the tables and a handful of picnic benches overflowed with students from our high school. Everyone who was anyone would rather gather here than anywhere else in town.

Our small town just outside of Salem had a quaint charm. For one, most stores and restaurants seemed to be stuck in Halloween mode and thus named their businesses appropriately. Even though I'd lived here my whole life, I still thought it was a kind of lame to forever be in Halloween town. Even our Easter celebrations took on a spooky atmosphere, and let's not even talk about Christmas—or shall I say Yule, as some people here preferred to call it.

Eye of Newt was owned by a guy named Newton Savage who supposedly lost his eye after a witch took it for a spell. That was, of course, absolute bullshit, since he clearly had both eyes and just wanted to sound interesting to newcomers.

We waited in line to place our order. That was the only downside to summer. People would much rather drink something cold than be at the other coffee shops. Well, the young ones, anyway. I couldn't blame them. Newt's place just had that amazing vibe that made you *want* to be here.

The room was decorated in multicolor, adorned with geometric shapes on the accent walls. Steampunk-styled lights hung from the high ceiling, creating the illusion of a bigger space, while the flaming light-bulbs gave the place a cozy atmosphere.

As we moved closer to the counter, the sounds became more noticeable—the clinking of glass and plates, the churring of the blenders, and the occasional thick whir of the frothing machine for those who wanted some caffeine and cream in their drinks.

"If it isn't my favorite customers. What will it be?" Newt sparked up the conversation as Mae and I finally got to the front of the line.

"I will have the Bubbling Cauldron, and she'll have the Death By Chocolate," Mae ordered, handing over a twenty.

"Hey, who said you can order for me?" I asked, pretending to be mad.

She put her hands on her hips and turned to me. "Well, you always take forever to order, and I know strawberry-chocolate with cream is your favorite."

She wasn't wrong.

As we stepped away from the counter to make way for others to order, the array of smells wafted over me. Coffee brewed in the corner and baked goods steamed in their glass cupboard, sending the absolutely delicious scent of cinnamon through the air. If I concentrated, I swear I could smell the fresh flowers on the tables accompanied by the faint odor of bleach. Every now and then, the chime of the door caused some of the customers to look up and see if one of their friends were joining the party.

"So, how many times is it now?" Mae asked, bringing me out of my sensory overload.

I frowned at her, unsure what she was talking about, when her gaze darted to the phone in my hand.

The screen lit up as yet another text from Ryker came through.

Where are you?

"I swear this man is going to send me to an institution early." I grabbed my phoned and sent off a quick text to let him know I was fine. Placing the phone back in my satchel, I avoided Mae's gaze and stared around the juice bar.

"He's just protective."

"I beg to differ. I don't need protection, I'm not a little kid anymore. Besides, nothing ever happens this town."

"There are things out there that you don't understand."

Before I could ask her what she was talking about, she headed to the counter and picked up our order before they even called out our names.

I mulled over her words and what they might mean. There had always been something different about Mae—like the way she knew things before it happened; her impeccable knowledge of the supernatural, which I might shrug off as Ryker's doing; and let's not even talk about the way she sometimes looked at someone while muttering to herself.

I watched her pass the array of chairs stacked around a few small bar tables that had been dragged together by the group of people. Most of the girls were seated on the stools and the guys were standing around, making jokes and fist-bumping each other as they made a point.

This was where we all came to be equal. The footballers made jokes with the nerds who played D&D in the corner, their board set on the coffee table as they sprawled on the sofas surrounding it. Some jocks even attempt to learn the game, but most of them give way to defeat not long after.

Artists and bookworms shared the wall filled with intricate statues and books, making small talk about which artistic method was best. As people passed me, some of their conversation drifted toward me, and it reminded me why I loved this town of ours. Yeah, you got the occasional dickhead, but most of the time we accepted each other, quirks and all. Or perhaps I should say warts and all, seeing as I was in a permanent episode of *Hubie Halloween*.

I was so entranced that when a car honked outside, I nearly fell onto my ass.

Clutching my chest to keep my heart from hammering through it, I looked through the glass windows to see what the commotion outside was all about. It seemed like a group of kids had jaywalked over the road without looking for cars and a black sedan nearly ran them over. Nothing weird in the occurrence, but something felt off about the car.

The car's windows were tinted to the point where you couldn't even see the driver. It was unmarked, but it might just have meant that it was a new car. The only thing I could make out were the silhouettes of whoever was in the car. I didn't know why, but I could have sworn that the driver was watching me, like they could see through the crowd inside the packed juice bar.

I tried to make out more details when Mae came waltzing to my side with our smoothies.

"See something interesting?"

I took my drink from her. "No, not really. I'm probably overthinking it."

She took a sip from her straw, watching me intently. The look in her eyes told me she didn't believe me. Taking a sip of my own drink, I nearly flinched at the coldness of the crushed ice.

The sweet chocolate touched my tongue before the somewhat sour taste of the strawberries. It tasted like someone had frozen chocolate-covered strawberries, then dipped them in sweet cream. The slight tinge of chili also came through. Newt had added his 'secret ingredient' to the mix, which wasn't all that big a secret since he always bragged that chili gave chocolate that extra, unexpected zap. It sounded disgusting, but somehow, he made it work.

"Come, we have lots to do." Mae nodded toward the door and I followed along behind her. Mae held the door open for me, and I stepped outside to the sound of screeching tires. The black sedan that had honked at the kids was now barreling down the road, away from the juice bar. A shiver ran up my spine and into my hair, but I shrugged it off. It was probably just from the cold of the shake.

"So, Newt said he's thinking of doing quiz nights and karaoke nights, you know, to liven things up a bit," Mae said, taking a sip of her juice as we headed in the direction of the bookstore'

"Liven things up? How busy does he want the place?"

"Even though the afternoons are packed, the nights are kind of dull. He suggested that 'it will give the kids something to do,'" she mimicked him, pushing out her chest in an imitation of Newt's ego.

"Hope he knows what he's getting himself into." I smiled as I thought about all the terrible renditions I've heard of every karaoke song in the world. "It might just force him to chase everyone away at five and lock up."

Our conversation died down, and we walked the streets in silence, sipping our juices in the blazing heat of summer. Luckily, the trees lining the sidewalks provided the perfect shade to prevent us from boiling to a crisp.

The atmosphere around town felt electric as students of every age made their way down the streets. Some rode their bikes while others glided around on their hoverboards.

Shouts drifted through the park as younger kids chased each other around, dodging the ball with which the older kids were playing. It was the perfect day to be surrounded by cheerful people. Even the young lovebirds walked hand in hand, making googly eyes at each other.

"Ugh," I muttered before realizing that I was displaying my annoyance out loud.

"What?" Mae asked.

"Huh? Sorry, just thinking out loud at how annoying the couples in this place can be."

"So now what, you don't like love?"

"It's not that I don't fancy the idea of feeling so super stoked to be around someone, but just thinking of having someone around *all* the time . . . I don't know, I guess that's why I'll be single forever."

Mae shot me a look full of fake shock, then jumped ahead of me and whipped out her phone. Before I knew what she was doing, she started speaking.

"Hey, all you wonderful people! Hope you are all having an amazing time. School's out, the sun's out, but there's another thing we need to get out." She turned around to face me, turning her phone's camera to face me.

"This is my absolute gorgeous friend, Amy. She seems to think that she's so full of shit, that she will never have a boyfriend."

"I am not—" I started to protest, but Mae just carried on with her live feed.

"If any of you amazing guys out there are interested, comment on the feed and show her some love. Trust me, this one will be worth it." She started moving around me with the phone, sticking it into my face.

"Just look at those amazing green eyes and those red locks—you won't get that in any salon." She moved behind me. "And don't get me started on this sexy ass of hers. Seriously, she could make a Brazilian butt lift jealous." Without even thinking, I tried to cover my ass so it wouldn't be on display to all her followers.

"So. hotties, make your presence known. Who knows, maybe you could be the lucky one to take this little ray of sunshine out on a date."

The mention of going on a date made my stomach drop. I grabbed her phone before she could end the live feed and turned the camera to focus on me.

"Ignore what this crazy woman just said. She's off her meds and delirious and—"

"I'll have you know I am very stable at this point in time."

"Then why the hell are you trying to set me up with the internet?"

Mae took the phone and came into view on the camera, holding her phone at arm's length so we could both fit in the shot. "Because you are amazing and need to be reminded of that."

"That's why I have you." I planted a kiss on her cheek, knowing full well that I would not be winning this battle.

"Ah, thanks, babe, but I don't swing that way." She addressed her unseen audience again, "But if any of you do, though, hit me up—"

"Or not," I interrupted, but Mae just bumped my shoulder with a smile plastered on her face.

"Hit me up and we'll see. Let the escapades of the bachelorette begin." She ended her feed and turned to face me. The enormous smile on her face said it all: I was going to regret this.

"Come on, we should probably get to the shop. The stock will not unpack itself," I said before she could say anything else.

We were nearing my uncle's bookstore, which he had opened many moons ago. The brown brick building came into view. The eye-catching sign read *WordCraft*, and an open book with a quill pen stood below the words, inviting people to come in and find their next best read.

As we crossed the street, my phone buzzed in my bag. Knowing full-well who it was, and that if I didn't answer the text immediately a string of incoming calls would soon follow, I opened my bag and started digging through it to find the annoying thing and reply to the other annoying thing. Mae was ahead of me as I struggled to find the phone in the mess of chewing gum, wallet, and papers. Why the hell do we women always have so much junk in their purses?

"AMY!" Mae's voice drifted toward me, and when I looked up, I noticed I had stopped in the middle of the road.

And a black sedan was hurtling towards me.

CHAPTER 2

*M*y blood ran cold. My feet refused to move. I stood like a deer caught in headlights. Time seemed to stretch out forever, but it all happened so quickly.

Mae was shouting. The car was barreling toward me with no sign that it would stop or even slow down. And all I could was stand there, unmoving, like a dumbass.

I never thought this was how I would die.

Something about the car seemed familiar. I struggled to figure it out, but in that moment, I knew this would definitely not be an accident.

A force from the side hit me hard, sending me to the sidewalk. As I hit the hot concrete, a weight settled on top of me, crushing my lungs as they clawed for air.

Stars flickered at the corner of my eyes when my head connected with the ground, sending newfound pain through my skull. I tried to focus. Tried to make sense of it all.

Did the car hit me? Was the impact the cause of being hurled through the air and hitting the road? Am I dying?

As those thoughts whirled through my mind, all I could think of was that dying wasn't as bad as I'd thought it would be. Then the weight on my chest shifted, easing the strain of breathing.

After a few gulps of air, my vision started returning and I heard muffled shouting that sounded like needles being embedded in my skull.

"Watch where you're going, asshole!" Mae's voice penetrated my foggy mind. I glanced to where I could hear her. Through my tunneling vision, I saw her standing in the middle of the road, yelling profanities at someone and hurling her juice cup at the person.

As she walked toward me, I noticed her legs were red and chafed and her eyes were filled with concern.

She knelt in front of me and helped me into a sitting position. "Are you okay?"

I winced at the searing pain in my head. "What the hell happened?"

"Some dickhead nearly ran right over you with his shiny new toy. Some people shouldn't be allowed to drive!" She yelled the last part even though the car was long gone. "C'mon, let's get you inside." She helped me to my feet and across the street to the bookshop.

Fumbling with the keys, Mae opened the door and shuffled me inside. The store smelled of old books and dust. Faint light drifted in from the half-open shutters, casting shadows between the rows of shelves.

After Mae locked the door behind us, she led me to one of the couches strategically placed so anyone could grab a book and unwind while reading.

"Sit here while I grab the medical bag from the back."

I nodded, and she slipped through the door to the storage room behind the counter.

Without her, the silence of the room was deafening but also tranquil, as if the unread stories on the shelves were whispering for me to read them, to fall within their pages and get lost outside of reality, even if only for a while.

Posters of famous quotes from the best authors adorned the walls—some were motivational while others were lines from books that gave the reader some introspection on the way they saw the world.

Mae came back carrying the red-and-white bag, already rummaging through it. She took a seat next to me and set the bag, a towel, and a bottle of water on the couch between us.

"Let's get you cleaned up a bit." She opened the water and wet the towel.

I gasped when she touched the wound on my head.

"Sorry," Mae said as she tried being gentler.

With every dab of the wet cloth, the pain seemed to subside. But then she used the disinfectant. As soon as the gauze hit the tender area, a few choice words escaped my lips before I could even think.

"Mother Ducker!"

"Breathe. It will be over soon."

"Tell that to my body," I said through clenched teeth. The disinfectant burned like she'd poured saltwater on an open wound.

"It doesn't look deep, so I don't think you'll need stitches. I'll just tape it so that it can heal better." Mae packed away the array of medical supplies and opened a roll of adhesive bandage. Cutting off a piece, she tenderly placed it on the cut.

"Thanks." My fingers automatically drew to the spot on my head.

"No problem. Glad it was just a bump and a scratch and nothing worse."

"You're telling me. If being sideswiped feels this crap, I don't want to know how bad the real knock would have been."

Mae gathered the things and went to put them away. When she came back, I was still lounging on the couch.

"Are you just going to sit there, or are you actually gonna do some work?" she asked, her hands perched authoritatively on her hips.

Looking behind her, I saw the stack of boxes I hadn't noticed when we first came in. With a sigh, I got to my feet.

"Where do you want me?"

"We need to unpack these boxes, cross reference them with the invoice and then shelve them."

"Is that all? What about grooming the flying unicorns?"

"They are actually called pegasus, unless they are unicorn-pegasus then they are called Alicorns."

"I was being sarcastic."

"I know, but I was not. Now start unpacking the boxes and you might actually learn something from them."

"Yes, Mom." I knelt at the boxes and started opening them.

"It's Boss Mom, thank you." Mae stuck her tongue out at me and grabbed the clipboard.

The next hour was spent taking the books from the box, reading off the name so Mae could double-check it on her list, then putting it in the genre pile on the floor, which we—-meaning *me*—would eventually pack away on the relevant shelf.

I picked up a book in the fourth box I had opened and read the title out loud.

"*The Element Encyclopedia of Signs and Symbols.*"

"Check," Mae commented. "That's actually a great read. Put it with the esoteric group."

"Great read? What's so interesting about signs and symbols?" I asked as I placed the book in the 'magical' group, as I'd dubbed it.

"Well, for one, signs and symbols not only tell us a lot about the past, but it opens a doorway to reveal things that you never knew existed."

"Oh, really? Like will I use—" I paused as I opened the book"—this thing to make myself invisible?" I pointed to a symbol that looked like a Viking-style snowflake, with a name I was never even going to attempt to say.

"That is a runic stave, and a dangerous one. It's said there's no counter stave for that rune, so if done right, you'd be invisible for all eternity."

"And here I thought it'd be a fun case of hide and seek," I said, putting the book back on the pile. "How do you know so much about this shit?"

"It was kind of drummed into me at a young age, which I guess makes me the perfect candidate to work here. Can't have a store manager with no intellect on their books."

We continued with our routine for a while, and when the last box was unpacked and captured, I got to my feet and stretched out my aching muscles.

"Okay, so, I'll grab the non-fiction and kids' books while you pack away all the esoteric things."

I looked at the piles on the floor and sighed. "Why do I get the most things to do?"

"Because you're a helper, plus you owe me for saving you from that car." Mae picked up her pile and walked off toward the shelf.

I glared at her for a few seconds and stuck my tongue out at her.

"I saw that!" she hollered from across the store, not even turning around.

"No, you didn't. You just know me too well," I called back as I picked up the first of many piles of what could only be classified as New-Age crap.

Making my way to the corner section of what my uncle had decided would make for the best energy flow, I placed the books on the shelf before setting each individual title in its right place.

There were so many themes on this shelf, it was no wonder that the people who usually came in here stood for hours, not knowing what to pick. The books ranged from dream interpretations, crystal healing, to magic in the ancient art scrying.

Who the hell would even believe this crap?

I wouldn't say that I was a cynic at all. I mean, our town was its own Mystic Falls without Damon Salvatore, of course, but magic? How could one believe in something that was not there? Something that just didn't exist?

I could understand the need for religion, to some extent. People needed to feel close to something. They needed to know that somewhere out there, a cosmic being watched out for them. It helped them sleep at night and be better people, but still . . . Relying on something without knowing with infinite assurance that it was actually there? No, thank you.

"Stop being such a cynic, Amy," Mae's voice drifted through the racks.

How the hell did she always know what I was thinking?

"How the hell?"

"I know you. You're busy looking over every book and wondering how people can believe in something unseen."

"Get out of my head, woman." I smiled as I packed away the last of the first stack of books.

"Can I ask you something?"

"Shoot."

"Do you believe in the wind?"

"What does that have to do with anything?"

"Just answer the question. Do you believe that the wind is real?"

I thought about her peculiar question but decided to answer honestly. "Well, yeah."

"How do you know that the wind is real if you cannot see it?"

I thought it over for a while. "You can see the wind blowing."

"Wrong. You can't physically see it. The effects the wind causes, the rustling of the leaves, the tornados cascading across the landscapes, sure, but you don't physically see it."

I knew she was far from done. Mae had a tendency to carry on until she'd made her point.

"Do you think love is real?" she asked again, coming out of the stack as I picked up my second pile of books.

"Really? Are we going to do this?"

She merely raised an eyebrow.

I walked to the shelf and plopped the books on top of the stack before turning around.

"Okay, fine. Let me guess. You can't see love but you can see the effects it has on people?" I challenged, my hand placed strategically on my hip, daring her to tell me I'm wrong.

"Why, aren't you a fast learner?" Sarcasm dripped from her lips as she mocked me. "Not only do you see the effects, but like the wind, if you experience it, you will feel it."

"What are you trying to do? Make me fall in love with the idea of love? Go back to your cave, cupid, and leave me be." I smacked her with the back of the book in my hand.

She giggled as she stepped behind the shelf again and started singing to herself.

It was only after I smacked her that I realized the book I'd hit her with was titled *"Into the Unknown: Understanding What You Cannot See."*

Well, isn't that a bit serendipitous?

I ignored the conversation as I stuffed the stupid book into its place. It felt like the universe was trying to tell me something. I hated being the butt of such jokes. Mae had probably given me this genre on purpose, knowing the topics would annoy me.

I finished shelving the books, then went to grab the last stack. Something outside the window grabbed my attention, and I glanced up.

A black sedan was parked at the corner of the road. Dark tinted windows, no license plate in sight. The sight of the car hollowed out a pit in my stomach. What were the odds that the car from the juice bar and the car that almost ran me over was now sitting on the corner outside the store?

On a normal day, I would have thought nothing of it except that the car seemed out of place—almost as if it had a dark presence that screamed to be noticed.

Now I sound like Mae with all her Ghandi insights.

I shook the thoughts from my head and continued my work, the sedan never far from my mind.

After I had finished, I went back to the window and looked outside again. The sedan stood in the blazing sun, watching me, taunting me. Almost daring me to do something. The shadowy figures inside made my stomach churn.

"Mae?"

"Yeah?" she answered, hardly lifting her gaze from her work.

"Can you come over here real quick? I think I might be losing my mind,"

"Oh, honey, that would entail that you actually have one."

When I didn't answer with a snarky comeback, she came out of the shelves and walked toward me.

I pointed at the vehicle. "Isn't that the same car as earlier?"

She stood in silence, studying the car. "Son of a bitch." She walked to the door, pulled it opened, and stalked to the car before I could even comprehend what was going on.

There was such vehemence in her stride that I winced as she drew closer. I heard her yelling, but I couldn't make out what she was saying. But whatever it was, it worked. The headlights came on as the car roared to life. Before Mae could come close to the vehicle, tires screeched, and the car sped off away from the store.

What the hell was that all about?

Mae stalked back to the store, anger and something else I couldn't decipher showing on her face. Something was up, and it wasn't just the fact that I almost got run over. Something else was brewing.

She marched into the shop and stormed straight to the counter, plucking her bag from under the counter.

"Mae, what's wrong?" I asked, looking over my shoulder as if the answer might be behind me.

She ignored me as she rummaged through her bag and pulled her phone from one pocket. Her nails tapped at the screen so hard that I was afraid she might crack the screen. A second afterward, she put the phone to her ear. Without even saying hello, Mae muttered three brief words.

"They are here."

CHAPTER 3

"Who's they?" I wanted to know, but Mae just turned her back on me and continued her conversation.

"Yes, I'm sure. The car almost trampled her." She walked back to the front window and peered outside. "I didn't think it was important. I thought it was just an asshole who couldn't drive."

I was becoming even more confused with each breath.

"No, not anymore. They sped off when I went to confront them." She pursed her lips. "Are you sure?" She turned to me and smiled half-heartedly. "I understand. I'll tell her." She disconnected the call and walked up to me. "Ryker wants you home. Now."

She took me by the shoulders and basically forced me out the door. I kept protesting, asking questions about what was going on, why was she speaking to my uncle and who the 'they' were she was talking about, but it all fell on deaf ears.

"What's going on?"

"You need to go home right now. Ryker will explain everything." She shoved me out the door and locked it behind me. Speechless, I stood on the curb, not knowing what the hell is happening. I turned around, wanting to confront Mae with more questions. But even the blinds in the shop had been drawn.

I knocked on the door, yelling her name, but it was as if she just disappeared.

"Mae! Open the door! C'mon, I don't even have my bag!" I shouted. I probably looked like a lunatic.

Suddenly, I felt a weight on my shoulder, like someone putting their hand on my shoulder, but when I turned my head, there was no one there. The only thing that was there, however, was the sling bag I had just been yelling about.

I must be losing my mind.

I adjusted the bag until it sat comfortably, then started toward my house, making sure to triple-check the road before I crossed it.

It was late afternoon, but the sun still blazed from behind the trees. Most of the children had gone home, with the exception of a few teenagers roaming about.

My mind reeled with the conversation Mae had on the phone and her very peculiar attitude toward me. Like, what was that? Had I pissed her off somehow? Was there something she wasn't telling me? And what the hell was Ryker's role in this?

I walked down the road close to the park, thinking over everything that was bothering me. My uncle Ryker had been part of my life for as long as I could remember. I never knew my mom—she died in a car accident when I was a year old, and Ryker never talks about her. He didn't know my father, and he didn't really care much. Ryker believed that any man who would leave a woman pregnant with his child was not worthy of the title of father. So, it kind of irked me that he might be keeping secrets from me. Especially since he bombarded me with continuous questions about my whereabouts every freaking half hour.

I was so distracted by my thoughts that I hardly noticed a car rolling down the road behind me at a snail's pace. If I hadn't looked behind me when I crossed the road, I wouldn't even have seen it.

That eerie feeling washed over me again. The same feeling I'd had when I first saw the car at the juice bar, when I saw the same car at the bookstore.

This was no coincidence.

I started jogging, hoping the sedan would realize that I was on to it. Maybe it would leave. No such luck, though. As I picked up my pace, the vehicle sped up.

We didn't live far from the bookstore, but it felt like miles at that moment.. I just needed to pass around the park, then I'd be home free. Ryker had always warned me about the vastness of the park at this time of day, saying that strange things happened when no one was looking. But I didn't really have much of a choice. My only options were to go around the park and have these creeps stuff me into their trunk, or to cut through the park and hope I'd lose them.

The fear in my heart made my decision for me as they came within striking distance.

I skidded to a halt and bolted into the park, hoping they wouldn't follow. The screeching tires and the sound of doors slamming told me I wasn't that lucky.

What was up with these people?

There was shouting behind me, but I didn't want to look. I'd seen this in movies—the protagonist being chased and looking behind her, only for her feet to betray her and for her to fall on her face, giving the bad guys the advantage of creeping up on her.

There was no way in hell I would become a statistic today.

I forced my feet to move faster, forced my burning lungs to take in more air, forced my body to push past the ache in my side. At the speed I was running, there was no way they would catch up.

I hoped.

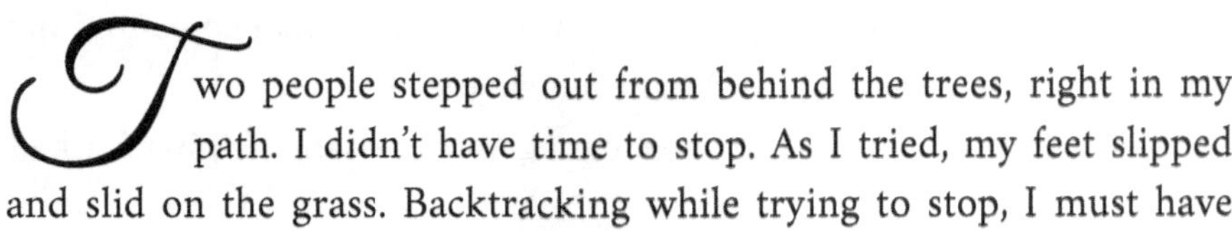

Two people stepped out from behind the trees, right in my path. I didn't have time to stop. As I tried, my feet slipped and slid on the grass. Backtracking while trying to stop, I must have looked like a gazelle on ice. My balance faltered as my feet struggled to gain traction.

I tripped and fell to the ground as my assailants came closer. How had they gotten ahead of me? Maybe there were more people in the car than I'd thought? Had the car driven ahead and dropped these two off so they could cut me off?

I slid backwards, trying to get away from the two in front of me, when my theory was confirmed. My back hit something hard, and a hand grabbed my hair, yanking me to my feet. A scream escaped me as I reached up to grab at the hands entangled in my hair.

"You shouldn't play with the toys," the creep behind me said as he threw me to the center of the group that had formed around me.

"Odd, I thought that was exactly what you did with toys." The one guy laughed, and it gave me the creeps.

Tears welled in my eyes from the searing pain left on my scalp.

I risked a glance at my attackers, hoping that if I survived today, I might identify them in a lineup, or at least give the cops something to go with.

Four men and one woman.

How could a woman allow something like this to happen to another woman?

They were all wearing black. Black tops, black pants, and black combat boots. They looked like the Serpents from *Riverdale*, but at that moment they seemed more dangerous than the Archie-comic imitations.

When one of the men moved toward me, a glint of something shiny caught my eye.

No.

A gun.

I looked around to the woman, hoping my pleading eyes would play on her sympathies and that she would snap out of the spell these men had cast on her, but my pleas were wasted on her. The woman was sporting a silver blade.

Fear triggered my fight-or-flight response and since I didn't know how to fight, I settled for the latter.

I jumped up and started running in a direction I thought held the least resistance, but one of the assailants quickly snatched me up.

"Where do you think you're going?" He sneered at me as he grabbed my arms, turned me around, and pushed me to the center again. I landed hard on my knees and could feel the burn of flesh being ripped from my hands as I scraped them on the hard ground.

"Aw, baby wants to play." The woman's laugh sent chills through my entire body.

Tears streamed down my face as I looked up at them.

"What do you want?" I asked, sounding much braver than I felt.

"Oh, not much. Just you." One of the men knelt in front of me, gripping a lead pipe. His pupils were so enlarged that I could barely see the green of his irises. Something wasn't right with these people, and I wasn't just talking about their thirst for young blood.

Bile threatened to rise in my throat, but I swallowed it down. No way in hell was I going to give them the satisfaction of humiliating myself.

Then something else happened. Heat started radiating from my hands. At first, I thought it was from the collision on the ground, but this didn't feel like a scrape or a bruise. This felt different.

The sensation started as heat, rising from my arms, creeping to my cheeks. It was soon accompanied by a tingling feeling. Like pins and needles.

Yet, it felt different. *I* felt different.

"She's channeling!" one attacker said, but I couldn't pinpoint which one.

The heat coursed through me like a hot branding iron down my throat.

"Stop her!" yelled another man.

I could sense them coming closer, but I could no longer see. Blinding white light illuminated my hands and spread to my arms.

As the heat in my body increased, the light became brighter.

I could hear shouting from all around me but couldn't make out the words, though from the tone of their voices they sounded worried and afraid. But why would they be worried? These fucknuts didn't give a rat's ass about me. And they had no reason to fear me, either.

My mouth moved of its own accord, forming words I had never uttered in my life, but I still made no sound. It felt like I wasn't in control of my body or my actions anymore.

A rapid pulsing started in my veins as the heat overtook the tingling. I wanted to scratch at my arms. To make this feeling stop. To stop the light burning within me, so I could see again, but something told me to let it all go. To release the power that was building inside.

I sat up on my knees, lifting my hands and opening to whatever was harnessed within me.

"Fuck!" The shout penetrated the noise in my head as the blinding white light became too brilliant and the power too intense for me to contain any longer.

Pulses radiated from me as I opened myself to the sweet release of what I could only assume was power. A scream so terrifying I didn't even realize was mine echoed through me, yet my voice vibrated with the intensity of it.

The pulsing vibration exploded along with the heat. The build-up felt like a bomb being compressed and finally giving way to the pressure. Light and heat escaped me, rippling through the park, leaving nothing in its wake.

It felt glorious—the feeling of immense superiority, of not being able to hold back, of letting go. Of giving in to your darkest desires.

The power subsided, drawing back the light to within me. The itching vibrations became a murmur, a humdrum of electricity as my vision darkened.

The last thing I saw was a silhouette running toward me.

CHAPTER 4

My head ached as my conscious mind started coming to. I wished for the darkness to claim me again. The pain was excruciating. When I stirred, I noticed I was lying on something firm but soft.

Groaning, I moved and immediately regretted it. It felt like a truck or a car hit me . . . wait, car. The images of what had happened ran through my mind.

A black sedan. It had stalked me, chased me. I'd run into the park to get away. There were guys . . . no, wait, four guys and a woman. They wanted something from me. I remembered their weapons. Their taunting. The light. The pulsing sensation.

"It's okay. You're okay." A soft voice drifted through my consciousness. It sounded familiar, yet I didn't recognize it. Was it a memory, or was someone here with me? The thought that someone was close to me after being attacked sent a bolt of panic straight into my heart. My breathing became rapid, fear gripping my chest.

"Amunet, you're safe now. No one can hurt you," the voice said again.

As hands gently touched me in comfort, my eyes flew open and I sat upright, ready for a fight. It took a while for my vision to adjust to my surroundings. When realization set in, I found myself on a couch inside a house. Inside my house. Pain shot through my body, forcing me to lie down again.

Stars danced across my vision. The pounding in my head felt like a jackhammer going to town inside my skull. Nausea swept over me as everything from the last few hours settled in my core.

I barely had time to sit upright when a bin was handed to me. My stomach heaved, forcing out everything until nothing remained but bile. It was almost as if my body wanted to rid itself of all the events that had taken place. All the fear, the panic, the emotions that came with it, all wanted to be expelled.

When I was sure that nothing else would come up, I lay back down and closed my eyes, placing my arm over my eyes in hopes that it would ease some of the pain. Sweat dotted my forehead as fever chills set in.

Footsteps echoed as whoever was here left my side and stalked off. Taking the chance, I glared out from underneath my arm and saw the familiar figure of my uncle walking to the kitchen.

I could hear him mumbling to himself as clinking sounds emanated from the kitchen. I lay there and just stared at my surroundings. Orange curtains closed off the windows. The soft leather couch I lay on was near the opening. A dark brown coffee table matched the couch. Two smaller couches stood on the opposite side of the room. There was a fireplace in the corner, waiting to be lit.

The smell of toast drifted through the house as the kettle whistled. Footsteps soon followed, the sound of spoons hitting against the cups. He placed a tray with two cups of tea on the coffee table, along with a plate of toast, lightly spread with butter. My stomach growled like a hungry predator, and I realized I was starving.

"I made you some tea to ease the pain and some toast to settle your stomach," Ryker said as he helped me sit up straight.

I mumbled a "thank you" as he handed me the plate.

I took a bite of the crisp bread, my stomach welcoming the food. The coarse texture helped settle the queasiness. The toast scraped against the tenderness in my throat, and when I finally spoke, my voice was raspy.

"What—" I tried to swallow. "What happened?" I asked, taking another bite.

Ryker's eyes drifted to the floor, and he let out a sigh. I could see him contemplating on where to begin. His brow furrowed as the wrinkles around his gray eyes tightened. His lips thinned above his salt-and-pepper beard.

"After Mae phoned me, I knew something was going to happen. I just had a feeling. I wanted to shrug it off as me being paranoid, but there's a reason for my paranoia. My gut always told me the truth. I waited for you, knowing you were on your way. When you didn't arrive when I knew you should have, I called Mae again to find out if you were still there, because you weren't answering your phone.. The fear I felt when she said you'd left half an hour earlier . . .

"I found you in the park, on the ground, unconscious. My heart stopped for a moment when I saw you, but when I saw you were breathing, I was so relieved. I immediately brought you home."

I nodded, but he hadn't answered my question. He was hiding something from me.

"But what happened? How did you know where I was?"

"What do you remember?" he countered.

"I remember the car and that Mae had chased it off. She was acting weird and talking with someone on the phone—you, I guess, since she told me you wanted me home immediately and then chased me out of the bookstore. I started walking when I noticed the car behind me. At first, I thought it was a coincidence, until they sped up when I started running." I took a sip from the tea and felt the cloud around my mind clear as the pain started subsiding.

"I thought if I cut through the park they wouldn't follow, and that I could get home faster, but they followed me. The five of them cornered me. They seemed dark, like a storm cloud clung to them. I was scared, especially when they started pushing and pulling me around. They had weapons and wanted to hurt me." My breathing became rapid, Tears filled my eyes and streaked down my cheeks as I relived the fear.

"I don't know what happened. I must have imagined it after I hit my head, but I could have sworn I started glowing. My whole body lit up, and it felt like I was going to explode. A woman's voice called to me, telling me to let go. I don't know who it was, but I did what she said. I released all the emotions that were building inside me, and that was the last thing I remembered."

Ryker nodded, a sad smile pulling at his mouth. "Kaye. She helped you release the power. She knew the impact would call to me." He whispered the words so softly that I wasn't sure I actually heard it.

"Who's Kaye? And what impact?" I asked, then took another sip of the tea.

"The magical impact of your power. It's basically a radar to those of our world," he said, ignoring my first question.

"Our world? What are you talking about? And who is Kaye?"

"Kaye was my wife. She has been watching over you your entire life. Some days I can still hear her voice criticizing me as I make the tea." The sad smile lingered as his eyes became vacant at what must have been memories playing out in his mind.

"I didn't know you had a wife."

"She died many years ago, saving my life and your mother's." His tone suggested that whatever had happened had been heart-wrenching.

"If your wife, Kaye, died so long ago, how was she able to talk to me? Or am I just going insane?" I asked the question with a tentativeness in my voice, hoping I wouldn't exacerbate his sadness.

"For that story, we will need some more tea." He got up and took the tray back to the kitchen.

The effects of the tea kicked in, and I could no longer feel the headache or the stiffness in my bones. Thank goodness Ryker knew a thing or two about herbology.

I could hear more clinging of cutlery against the cups, and before I knew it, Ryker was back with two steaming mugs of tea.

"You are going to need more than a mere cup for this. I also put in something extra for calming and understanding." He handed me my mug and sat down on the coffee table. The smell of lavender, chamomile, and vanilla drifted into my nose as I took the first sip. The smoothness of the tea relaxed me almost instantly.

When he started by saying, "Amunet," I knew it was serious. He always used my full name when speaking to me, but his tone suggested things were about to get real.

"The day you were born, your mother, Samena, was ecstatic, to say the least, but she feared for your life. There are things in this world that you are not aware of, as I felt it would be easier for you to live a normal life. Not one where you had to look over your shoulder every minute of every day."

His words made no sense to me. Why would I be in danger?

"Your mother died protecting you when you were just a baby. She was attacked, as you were, but she did not have the same power that you possess. She fought so hard. Unfortunately, she just wasn't strong enough. Neither of us were." Tears rolled freely down his face as he recalled the memories.

"My daughter died trying to save you. She died so that I could get you to safety."

"Wait . . . daughter? But I thought you said my mother died?"

"She did. I have been keeping a secret from you, Amunet. One that you might not yet understand or even believe. Your mother was my daughter. I am not really your uncle, Amunet, but rather your grandfather. It was just easier to tell everyone I was your uncle than having to explain to humans who I really was."

"That's not even possible. You can't be my grandfather. You're, like, forty."

A genuine smile tugged at his lips. "Thank you for the compliment, but I am much older than you think."

"What, like fifty? Fifty-five?"

"More like four hundred, give or take a few years."

"Bullshit! That's impossible! No one can live that long." Did Ryker really think I was that gullible? That I would believe he was that old?

Unless he drank from the fountain of youth, which he didn't because that was a myth and myths don't exist.

"No *human* can live that long, but the Pure can."

"Human? So what, you're some kind of alien? That would explain some of your odd behavior."

"No, I'm no alien." He chuckled. "But I am a Pure. Drink your tea and let me explain."

I did as he asked and waited for him to speak.

"Back when the Earth was still young, the old gods roamed the world, keeping the balance between light and dark. They saw the potential of some souls and bestowed upon them the gifts of the celestials. These gifted souls contained the power of the gods, to an extent, and they were tasked to protect the balance of light and dark. Their mortality was extended in such a way that some would have thought them to be immortal. Because they exemplified the purest nature of what humans were capable of, they were known as the Pure.

"Through the millennia, these gifts were passed down to the descendants of these souls, who were then tasked to continue that balance of the world." He took a sip of his tea, and I did the same, trying to comprehend what his words meant. At this stage, I would write it off as going bonkers.

"By that time, the gods had all returned home, and the people forgot about the legends of the Pure, except for those who were descendants."

I sipped at my tea. How did any of this apply to my current situation?

"The Pure showed powers that could only be explained today as that of the movies. They could cast spells, draw on the elemental energies of the earth, and wield it to their advantage. Some Pures could even channel the powers of the ancient gods."

"You're saying that there are witches among us?"

"What I'm saying is that you, my dear Amunet, are the last remaining descendant of the Pure."

CHAPTER 5

"Whoa there, Sorcerer Mickey." I stood and paced around the room, trying to process. "You're telling me that I showed signs of power when I was attacked?"

"Not just signs, you were power incarnate."

"And that your dead wife of four hundred years ago, who by the way is my grandmother and you are my grandfather, communicated with me through the veil of the afterlife? And that not only am I not a normal person, I'm not even human? I'm, like, what? A glorified witch on steroids?"

"I wouldn't go so far as to say you're not human—" Ryker started.

"Really? Out of all the rambling, *that* is the part of the conversation you had to correct?" Exasperated, I fell onto the armchair, trying to wrap my head around the fact that he'd just admitted to not only being my grandfather, which I still doubted, but also that I was some sort of badass witch thing.

I really must have hit my head hard.

"I know it's a lot to take in—"

"A lot to take in? A lot to take in would be discovering I had a long-lost twin somewhere out there. A lot would be to tell me I was adopted.

28

This"—I gestured vaguely at him—"is just crazy talk. How the hell am I supposed to believe you?" I sat upright, getting ready to pace the room again to calm my mind.

But then something impossible happened.

Ryker sat at the coffee table with his hands outstretched in front of him. A small blue light appeared, highlighting his features. The next moment, a dolphin made entirely out of water, jumped off his hand, then landed back in his hands.

Stunned at what I was seeing, I could only stare, mouth agape. He continued with the show of sea creatures, each jumping out of the water in his hand and back again. When he was sure he'd made his point, the light in his hands dimmed until it was no more.

"That was . . ." I started, but words seemed to fail me. "How'd you—" How could I voice something I didn't understand? How could I describe something I'd only seen occur in movies?

"You already have the power within you, you just need to learn how to control it." Ryker smiled, but my eyes still felt like they were bulging out of my head. What he had just shown me should have been impossible, yet he'd sat there and demonstrated some weird David Blaine shit.

What was this really? Illusions? Holograms? Concussion? Magic? I struggled to comprehend this, to understand it. What he was telling me was going against my moral-realist mind. The one that told me that the glass wasn't half-full or half-empty, but that it merely contained liquid.

Clearly Ryker could see I was struggling to come to terms with this information, because he stood and put his hand on my shoulder, giving it a reassuring squeeze.

"Get some rest. Tomorrow will be a long day, and we have much to discuss." He bent and placed a kiss on my head, then headed to his room, switching off all the lights along the way.

*T*he next morning, I woke with some sore muscles, but that was about it. I shrugged off the previous night's conversation with my uncle as my mind trying to combat the stress and exhaustion.

No way what I had experienced was real.

I stalked to the kitchen for some breakfast and much-needed coffee. Ryker was already cooking. My stomach growled at the bacon-scented air.

"Morning, sleepyhead. Breakfast is almost ready."

His cheerful demeanor made me suspicious of his motives. I poured myself a cup of coffee from the coffee machine and sat down at the kitchen table.

The heavy scent of wild coffee beans filled me with so much joy that a normal person would think I hadn't had a cup in years. The warm liquid traveled down my throat, and a soft moan escaped my lips before I could help myself.

"That good, huh?" Ryker asked with a smile and mischief in his eyes.

I closed my eyes in enjoyment. "You have no idea."

The toaster popped, and Ryker set the toast on a plate. After dishing up some bacon and eggs, he placed the plate in front of me.

"Eat up, we have lots to do and discuss." Turning around, he dished up for himself and got comfortable across the table.

I eyed him carefully, but he pretended not to notice my scrutiny of his appearance as he dug into his breakfast. The brown hair streaked with a bit of gray, the salt-and-pepper beard trimmed to perfection, the slightest hint of crows' feet at the corners of his gray eyes . . . there was no way he was old enough to be my grandfather.

If that conversation had even happened.

"It did happen," Ryker muttered, taking a bite of his eggs.

"What?"

"Yesterday happened. Everything I told you did happen; it wasn't just a dream," he said nonchalantly, hardly making eye contact, as if he just told me the sky is blue.

"Forgive me for not believing you, but witches and magic just don't exist."

"Oh, it exists all right. It's as real as this very moment. It's as tangible as you and me."

"Then why the hell haven't I ever seen it?"

"Maybe you were looking, but you weren't really seeing."

"Okay fine, Yoda. If it all does exist, prove it. And no more Copperfield crap."

"Copperfield is an illusionist. It's usually what happens when humans want magic but weren't born with it, so they pretend to own it."

"So, you're saying David Blaine and Chris Angel are just illusionists? Have you even seen their performances?"

"I have. Blaine and Angel are both born of magical families, so they might have some powers, but they use that with illusion to entertain people. I will tell you everything later, but first, finish your breakfast. You'll need it."

And that was that. No more bantering. No more answering of questions. Just the two of us eating breakfast in silence. Every couple of bites, I looked over at Ryker, wondering if he was the one who had hit his head, or whether I was in a prank show.

My phone buzzed on the table while I contemplated the prank show, glancing around the kitchen for hidden cameras. Unlocking the screen, I saw I had a ton of unread messages.

I set down my fork and scrolled through it to see why I was suddenly so popular. A bunch of the messages were from Dakin, one of my best friends, asking me if I was okay and what had happened. Mae must have updated him on the events, so I sent him a quick message back saying that I was a bit shaken but was fine and that I would explain everything later.

The next couple of messages were all from Mae.

Are you home?

Sweets, where are you?

Ryker just phoned. Holy Shit, Aims! Call me when you get this.

Babes? I just want to make sure you are okay. Ryker never gives any details and I know you won't discuss what's on your mind with him.

AMUNET WICC!! Talk to me, for shit's sake!

Something told me I would be in the doghouse for a while. I pulled my courage up by its pants and typed out a response.

Hey, babe. Sorry, I'm only getting back to you now. I was out of it. Misplaced my phone and . . .

I didn't know what to say. That I wasn't in my right mind to talk? That Ryker was telling me a fairytale that he believed to be true? I typed the only thing that I could think of.

I'm sorry. I'm okay. Didn't mean to make you worry.

*W*ithin a few seconds, three dots highlighted our chat. As I waited for her text to come through, I drank the rest of my coffee and stood up for another cup. When I sat down, my phone buzzed again.

"You're pretty busy on that thing," Ryker said as he watched me intently over his cup of tea.

"Sorry. Mae's on my case and wants to know how I am."

"And? How are you this morning?"

"I don't really know. Everything feels normal, but it also feels as if I'm in a dream where nothing makes sense. Like I'm Alice roaming through Wonderland."

"It's only because you haven't processed it yet. Text Mae back, then join me in the living room. As I've said, we have much to discuss." Ryker stood and left the kitchen, taking his tea with him.

Mae: Ryker told me what happened. I'm so sorry. I should have gone with you.

Me: It's okay, I'm fine now. But Ryker does want to have a chat about something. Seems important. Chat later.

Mae: Okay, call me when you done.

I locked my screen and headed to the living room, cradling my cup in my hands. It felt like I was a kid, getting the talk about something I did wrong. Sitting down on the same couch as the night before, I waited for the talk of disappointment to come.

Ryker settled into the small armchair opposite me and stared at me, analyzing my body language as if to see how to start.

"What do you remember from yesterday?" he asked, drumming his fingers on the side of the couch.

I felt like I was being questioned to determine my state of mind.

I relayed everything I could remember from our conversation the day before. The stories he'd told me of the Pure and that they had celestial powers and were supposed to keep the balance between light and dark.

I also voiced my opinion that it was all bull and probably a prank set up by him or my friends because I was a non-believer of all things magical and mystical.

"You have a vivid imagination, even for a cynic." He laughed as he uncrossed his legs and sat forward in his chair.

"I'm not a cynic, I'm realistic," I replied, folding my arms over my chest, daring him to prove me wrong.

"And the difference is?" he countered, and by the look in his eyes, he knew he was right.

I uncrossed my arms and scooted in deeper into the couch. "You said we have things to discuss?" I mocked his tone from earlier, which made him chuckle.

"You are just like Kaye. Wearing your heart on your sleeve and never backing down." He smiled at me. A hint of sadness touched his eyes for only a moment, then he went back to his normal self again. "Last night I told you about the Pure—who they were and how they came to be. But I haven't told you about the dangers we face."

"Dangers? Like the attackers from yesterday?"

He nodded and clasped his hands in front of him. "Now, not all the Pure souls remained that way. In the 1600s, there was a soul that tasted power, more so than his celestial ones, and he wanted more. We are not entirely sure what made him turn, but he stepped over the line between light and dark. He became Tainted.

"This Tainted, Gorice is his name, had it in his mind that if he stole the souls of the Pure, he would receive their powers and become almighty. That was when he started to hunt them all down."

"Wait. You said his name *is* Gorice, not was."

"Yes. His soul was sent through to the ethereal and he has been roaming there, waiting for his opportunity to get the soul of the last Pure to reinstate his power and resurrect himself."

"Okay, but what about the ones who attacked me?" I asked, wondering what this would all mean to me.

"Those are Gorice's followers. Some of them are Tainted, but not many, but most of them are just witches and mages who went dark."

"But if Gorice is so dark, why would anyone follow him? Why would they turn?"

"Power, promises Gorice made that he would fulfill their darkest desires, and fear. People do strange things if they fear for their lives or the lives of those close to them."

"But why would they come after me? I have nothing they want." I suddenly felt small and exposed, and I shifted around until my legs were curled underneath me.

"That's where you're wrong, Amunet. You have everything they want. You are the last Pure, and they will stop at nothing until they have your soul."

CHAPTER 6

The realization of what he was saying hit me like a tidal wave.

"They attacked me because of who I am to them?"

"Yes. They didn't want to mug or torture you, even though I wouldn't have put it past them. They wanted your power. Your soul."

"Thanks for sugar-coating it," I snapped, suddenly enraged. "What will keep them from trying again?"

"Those won't, they're dead. But others will. That is why we need to start your training immediately." Ryker stood and paced to the fireplace. He lifted his hand and waved it in front of the wall above the fireplace, intoning words I didn't understand.

There was a low rumbling as the wall shifted and moved away, revealing a small crevice housing an enormous book. The second Ryker removed the book, the wall closed, and it was like there had never been an opening.

I studied the space, trying to see a line or even an indication that there was a mysterious hidden space above the fireplace, but nothing gave it away.

How was that possible?

Ryker sat next to me and placed the book on his lap, stroking it gently. "This is a grimoire. It contains every spell known to man and more." He handed me the book. "It also contains the tales of the past and foretellings of the future."

The book was lighter than it looked and was bound in a strong, dark leather, embellished with gold and gems with symbols I didn't recognize. As I brushed the cover, I felt the pulse of what I assumed was magic.

"We'll start with the smaller things—light levitation, creating fire, manipulating water and wind while getting in touch with the earth."

"That doesn't sound small, nor easy." I opened the book at a random page and just stared at the foreign words. My eyes widened. "How the hell am I supposed to know all of this?"

"Once you get control of your magic, you will no longer need the words. That's what makes us different from the normal witches. They need the words to cast the spells, we need the words until we control our power." He paged through the book, then stopped and pointed to the page. "These simplistic spells are written in Latin, the language of old. Once you understand them, you will understand your power."

"What does this mean?" I asked, pointing to a word.

"Fire. You use it to either cast fire to a place or hold it in your hand."

"How do you pronounce it?"

"You can either call to fire or you can ignite something like a candle," he said as he took the small candle from the table and placed it in front of me. "If you want to ignite the candle, look at the wick of the candle and imagine the flicker of the flame start up and continue. Once you have that image in your mind, you must speak the word with intention. The word for ignite is *Ardescat*."

I scooted closer to the edge of my seat and stared at the candle. I imagined what it would look like when it was lit. I imagined the small flame dancing as a slight breeze moved it around.

"*Ardescat*," I spoke, but nothing happened. I looked at Ryker, but he just nodded and indicated I try again. I took a deep breath, cleared my mind and envisioned the same image. I spoke the word again, and I could feel a tiny tingle dancing over my body. When I opened my eyes, there was a flame.

"You're shitting me! You lit the candle while my eyes were closed."

"I did not. You channeled your power, and the elements obeyed."

"I don't believe you."

"Hold out your hand, palm facing up. Envision a ball of fire dancing above your palm and say, *Incendia*."

"Whoa, whoa, whoa. I'm not burning my hand to prove a point."

"The second goal of being a Pure is to know your craft and believe in it. If you doubt in your magic, nothing will happen. If you fear your magic, things will go wrong. Have the confidence a child would have in a superhero cape."

I nodded, but I was wary of the injuries I'd sustain if I actually made a ball of fire dance on my palm. I lifted my hand and closed my eyes, trying to visualize what Ryker had told me. Once I was confident that I had the perfect image, I uttered the word.

Immediately, heat rose, but it wasn't from the palm of my hand. I opened my eyes and saw that the fire ball I had envisioned wasn't there. The grimoire was ablaze!

"Shit!" I jumped up, letting the book fall to the floor. As I was about to stomp on it, Ryker waved his hand over the book and the flames dissipated. He picked it up and turned it around. Not a spark was to be found, and the pages looked as if they had never seen fire.

"How—" I gaped, inspecting the pages, paging through the book. Not a single mark.

"The grimoire is protected by magic so it cannot be damaged." He mentioned it as if it was no secret.

"Why did the book catch fire? Did I do something wrong?"

"In a way."

My mood sank.

"The only thing you did wrong was to fear. You believed in a way that you can do it, but you were afraid that you would get hurt. Remember, the magic that comes from you cannot harm you."

I nodded. I struggled to believe him. It would take me a while to get the hang of it, to believe in myself and my abilities. It still felt like this was all a dream and that I would wake up soon.

"I think it might be best if we took our training sessions outside. To lessen the damage. Or until you start believing and stop fearing," Ryker said as he closed the book.

~

"I'm trying!" I yelled after my umpteenth attempt at trying to lift a rock off the ground without touching it. We'd been at it for hours. Ryker thought it would be best to leave the fire practice until I had more control.

"You are letting your emotions get the better of you. Anything you attempt in a negative space will have a negative effect on your magic."

"Thank you for the obvious, Mr. Miyagi. I know this. You've told me the thirteen goals already. I'm just . . . tired, I guess."

"Maybe we should take a break. Get something to eat, maybe call Mae back like you promised this morning?" Ryker suggested.

Crap. I hadn't texted or called Mae and Dakin yet.

Ryker went into the house and left me alone. I grabbed my phone from the porch and dialed Mae's number.

"Finally! That must have been some talk," Mae answered without even a hello.

"Well, hello to you, too."

"How are you feeling?"

"I'm good, everything was just a lot to take in." I sat on the step as I wondered how much I could tell Mae. Ryker had said nothing about keeping this a secret, but he also didn't say that I could announce it to the world.

"I bet. Did Ryker say anything about your attackers or why they did what they did?" she asked, putting me on the spot.

"Not really. They are gone now, but he thinks they just wanted to rob me."

Mae was quiet, which was unusual, since she always had some kind of comment to make. I was half expecting something along the like of 'those assholes' or maybe even 'if I get my hands on them . . .' but nothing. I checked my phone for the signal, thinking that maybe we got disconnected, but she was on the line.

"A customer just walked in. Talk to you later."

Before I could answer her, she hung up. No goodbye or 'take care of yourself.' She was just gone.

"That's probably the weirdest conversation I've ever had with her." Sitting there in silence, Mae's weird vibes running through my mind.

I looked to the house to see where Ryker might be and decided to call Dakin. I hadn't spoken to him since school ended. Could that really only have been a day ago?

After a few rings, Dakin picked up. I could hear the smile in his voice.

"Well, if it isn't Jason Bourne,"

"Haha, very funny." A smile settled on my face. Talking to Dakin always made me feel better.

"So, how are you?"

"Can't complain. Actually, I can, but who listens anyway?"

"I do. I always do. So, what's up? What's troubling you?"

"I hate that you know me so well." I began telling him everything about the last day, leaving out the magic and Ryker's revelation, of course. He might just think that I was going mad. I even told him about Mae's odd behavior.

"Don't you think maybe she feels guilty about what happened?" he asked.

I loved how he always played the Switzerland card and made you think from the other person's perspective.

"What do you mean?"

"Think about it. She was with you when you almost got hit by the car. She was with you at the store when the same car stalked you, and she's the one who sent you home by yourself, which led to you being attacked. I think she feels terrible for not being with you. She's probably thinking that if she'd gone with you, nothing would have happened."

That made sense. I would have felt crap if our roles were reversed.

"But I'm okay now. Except for a few bumps and bruises, I feel fit as a fiddle."

"That might be true, but it still doesn't stop her from feeling the way she does."

"You're right."

"Ain't I always?" he asked, and I could just imagine the smirk on his face.

"Okay, Obi-Wan, lie down before you hurt yourself."

He chuckled, which made me laugh.

"The force is strong with this one," he mocked in his best rendition of Darth Vader, and it only set me off with a fit of giggles.

Ryker came back and nodded that we should continue with my training.

"Hey, I got to go. Ryker's calling me. Talk to you later?"

"Don't let him be too hard on you," he laughed as he said goodbye.

I disconnected the call and went to stand in the backyard again with Ryker.

~

After a few more hours of struggling, I got the rock to waver on the table, but that was about it. Frustrated, I threw my arms up in surrender.

"I give up! This is hopeless. How am I supposed to protect myself if I can't even lift a damn stone?"

"Patience, my dear. All good things—"

"Come to those who wait. Yeah, yeah, I've heard all this crap before. What if I'm not the right one for this? What if the universe made a mistake in choosing me?" I said, voicing my frustration.

"What if you're right?" Ryker's comment caught me off guard.

"Excuse me?"

"Oh, you're excused. Maybe they chose the wrong person. Maybe you're not who I thought you were." His entire demeanor changed from guiding mentor to a super jacked-up asshole.

"Really?" I asked in disbelief.

"Maybe I never should have found you in the park yesterday. Maybe I never should have taken you in."

"Stop it!" His harsh tone stung.

"You know, I think life would have been better. Kaye never should have sacrificed herself to save the bloodline. You obviously aren't worth it."

"Shut up." Tears welled in my eyes. When had he become so mean?

"I don't know what I was thinking."

"Shut. Up," I said again, raising my voice. Heat surged through me, fed by my anger and hurt.

"If I hadn't let my daughter give her life to save you, she would still be here."

"I said, shut up!" I screamed, tears flowing freely down my face. The heat inside me blasted outward, sending a wave of energy at Ryker.

He flew backwards through the air before crashing to the ground. He huffed, and a grunt escaped him as he just lay there, unmoving.

I clasped my trembling hands over my mouth. I used my power on him. What had I done? His cruel words to me forgotten, I rushed to his side. When I touched him, his eyes flew open, and he gasped for air. He groaned when he tried to sit up.

"Now I know how the Tainted felt." He chuckled and winced, clutching his side.

"Ryker . . . I'm so sorry. I didn't think. I would never—"

He touched my cheek, rubbing a tear from my face with his hand.

"I know, sweetie. I was actually planning on it."

"What?"

"We weren't getting anywhere, and I needed to make you trigger your magic. I didn't mean any of what I said. I just used the words so your magic could surface. Didn't think that you would explode, though."

He laughed as he rolled to his side to get up. I wanted to hug him for being alive, but I also wanted to kill him for tricking me.

"I think training is done for today. I'll be right as rain by tomorrow." He walked into the house and that was that.

I was dumbstruck. How the hell did that actually happen?

I looked at my hands. Sparks of power lingered on my skin.

CHAPTER 7

Fire. Burning bright, blindingly white. The room was covered in it. At first, I thought I'd accidentally set flame to my room, but as I glanced around, nothing seemed familiar.

This wasn't my house, nor any other house I've ever been in. Were it not for the raging inferno around me, the room would have been small and cozy.

A figure engulfed in flames stood in the middle of the room. The crackling of embers emanated from him, the sickly scent of burning flesh surrounding us. He stared at me, as if the flames didn't bother him.

All I could see were his eyes. Dark and dangerous. They stared into my soul, but I couldn't look away. When he came closer, my breath caught in my chest.

Ryker.

Was this a premonition of what would come to pass? Would this happen to Ryker?

Even though the entity in front of me looked like him, something told me it was not Ryker. He was shrouded in darkness. The sense of evil struck me as he came closer still.

"Amunet," he whispered, reaching toward me. His voice sent shivers through my entire body.

Something was wrong. I just couldn't put my finger on what. I tried to step back, out of his reach, but the fire was encasing the walls. If I moved too much, I would get burned.

Yet he kept coming. Slow and menacing. Whispering my name as he reached out to touch me.

"My soul."

Another shadow figure stood in the fire. Even though this one was at the back of the room, the power radiating from them could be felt from where I stood.

"Gorice!" a woman's voice called out.

The Ryker lookalike in front of me stopped in his tracks. He turned around to look at the woman.

"No! She's mine!" He made a move to pounce, but the woman lifted her arms, and without a word, the burning man in front of me was pulled back toward her.

I woke in a cold sweat, fear hammering my heart so loud I thought someone was pounding on my door. As my eyes adjusted and my room came into focus, my breathing settled.

In my mind, I could still see the fire raging throughout the room. The smell of burning flesh scorched my nose. His face still vivid as the flames engulfed him, but the darkness roamed as if dancing with his torture.

The other shadow figure plagued me though. Why was she there? The fire had touched her, but it was as if the flames had merely danced around her magic.

Whoever she was, she seemed to be able to control the burning man to some extent. The name she spoke flashed through my mind.

Gorice.

A newfound fear came over me. He knew my name. He knew what I looked like. He wanted not only my soul, but he wanted revenge.

He was here, and he was coming. I knew it like I knew the sun would rise and set again today. An urgency set in, and I knew what I had to do.

I got out of bed, knowing there was no way I could get back to sleep. Not with the vision still so vivid that I could hear the crackling of flames and smell the burning flesh. I could even still feel the heat on my arms, as if I was standing by the fire.

I headed to the kitchen, where I made some chamomile milk, just like Ryker used to do. Just the thought of him made me shudder.

Why did Gorice look so much like Ryker? Maybe I was projecting his face into my dreams. They said you can't dream of someone you have never seen, so I probably made Gorice look like Ryker.

As the milk warmed up, I added some honey for sweetness and waited for the milk to boil. I poured it into a mug and went to sit on the couch in the living room.

The house was quiet. It felt like I should be doing more with my time, so I switched on the lamps and went over to the fireplace. I held my hand up in front of the hidden place, but Ryker hadn't shown me how to open the hidey-hole.

"Open Sesame," I said, hoping that it would be that easy, but the fireplace remained closed. "Abracadabra?" I asked, thinking that Ryker's fascination with magicians could be the key. Still, it remained closed.

I tried to rack my brain for more 'magic' words, but nothing came. A breeze shifted my hair, and a soft voice whispered, *"Apere."* I looked around but saw no one there. My gut told me to trust the voice, and so I did.

Placing my hand in front of the space, I repeated the word. *"Apere."*

To my delight, the stones shifted, revealing the grimoire in all its magnificent glory.

I could feel the humdrum of power vibrating within the book as I picked it up. I couldn't think that a few days ago I didn't know any of this was real, and now I didn't think I'd be able to go back to normal.

I sat back in the armchair and opened the book. The vibrations intensified, as if the grimoire were alive. The first few pages were stories written about the Pure and how they came to be, the thirteen goals of being a Pure as well as some encyclopedia entries on herbs, crystals, and colors—what they meant, how they worked and how one could harness their energies to increase spells.

No wonder Ryker enjoyed his tea. These herbs could be used for anything. Chamomile for calming, lavender for restfulness, peppermint and rosemary for energy and focus. The list was endless. Now his energy and Buddhist-calm made so much sense.

I came across some spells, the ones Ryker said was small magic. Even though these spells were small and simple, they could do a lot of damage, depending on your intentions.

Looking over the words, I decided to try one that would cause the least amount of damage.

"*Lux*," I whispered, not wanting to wake Ryker up, but nothing happened. I raised my hand, palm facing up, and envisioned the ball of light, then spoke the words again, but still no ball of light. Not even a spark.

Clear your mind, focus, believe.

That same whisper from earlier. The same one I'd been hearing since the attack in the park.

"Kaye?"

Ryker had told me she was always looking out for me, so why wouldn't it be her? My only answer was the slight breeze ruffling my hair. I took that as a confirmation. I closed my eyes and took a deep breath, trying to focus my mind on nothing but my intention.

When the tingling feeling in my hands started, I knew I had reached my magic. I spoke the word again with intense certainty, as if I knew it would work. I opened my eyes, and a ball of light floated a few inches above my hand.

Wonder and excitement filled me.

I did it! I finally created something with intent.

I poked at the ball with my other hand and the light exploded into hundreds of smaller lights, imitating stars. They hung in the air, illuminating the room.

This was so cool. I imagined them dimming away like fireworks, and the light obeyed my thoughts. Slowly, each light star sparkled away, fading into nothingness, leaving me again with the lamps as my only source of sight.

I tried it again, visualizing the light floating above my hand as I repeated the word *Lux*. The light formed, glowing in the air.

I let it fade out again, then repeated it again and again. When I was confident that I had the hang of it, I decided I wanted to try and see if I could conjure it without the words.

Holding up my hand and envisioning the ball, I made my intention known without saying the spell. To my amazement, the magic within me obeyed, and the light started taking shape.

Awed, I looked how a swirl of sparks came and formed out of nothing, the small ball of light hovering in midair. The white danced with a hint of blue as it glowed in front of me. The beauty was mesmerizing. No wonder people sought out this power.

I cast the light into the air, willing it to multiply and light up the living room as it had before. The magic complied. Before I knew it, the room was sparkling with balls of mystical light.

This achievement gave me a new sense of purpose as I took the book and paged to other spells. I tried a telekinetic one. Speaking the incantation, *Vitae*, I waited to see if my intention on the couch cushion was strong enough.

Suddenly, the cushion was floating in mid-air, hovering over the couch. I wanted to see if I could move it across the room. At first, I let it go up and down a few times, then I shifted my eyes to the side so quickly that the cushion sped across the room, hitting one of the portraits hanging on the wall. The cushion fell to the ground with a loud thump.

"Shit," I whispered, waiting for the swinging portrait to either stop moving or crash to the ground. Luck seemed to be on my side as the picture settled and everything was silent.

"Okay, so not doing that again," I muttered under my breath, thinking about the damage I could have caused. Good to know I could move things around, though.

The next spell I decided to try was to turn a liquid into a solid and then undo the spell. I looked over at my mug. It was half-full.

Why the hell not?

"Aqua facient solida," I spoke my intentions to the mug, keeping my mind clear of any negativity.

It stunned me to see that my milk had hardened and become like ice. I picked up the mug, inspecting it.

The mug felt cool to the touch, the liquid inside solidified into ice. My chamomile milk was now an icicle. I held the mug in my hand as I looked at the reversal spell.

"Reverte! Reverte ad vestrum priorem statum."

I felt the tingle of magic move inside the cup as the ice turned into milk almost immediately. I tilted the mug to look inside, forgetting that it contained liquid.

"Shit." So much for being careful. The milk splashed on my pajama pants, leaving a large wet mark. It looked like I'd wet myself.

Placing the mug back beside me, I reverted to the book. This was definitely going to change my life. I spent the rest of the early morning hours working on various spells and committing them to memory.

It was hard enough to remember the normal things in my life, so I had to make a plan to memorize the Latin, or better yet, perfect the spell so I didn't need the words anymore.

As I paged through the grimoire, I came across more advanced spells that were long and needed candles, crystals, and a protective circle.

I made a mental note to ask Ryker about it when the time came, wondering why one would need a depossession spell.

CHAPTER 8

The enticing scent of oats and biscuits filled the kitchen as I poured boiling water into the teapot, knowing that Ryker would be here any second. I filled the two bowls with the porridge and placed it on the kitchen table next to the plate with cookies. Just as I set the butter and cinnamon sugar on the counter, Ryker stepped in, staring at the spread.

"Well, this is a surprise."

"I couldn't sleep, so I started breakfast. Want some tea?"

"That would be great, thank you."

I made my way to the pot and poured him a cup. Deciding to give him a bit of a shock, I focused on the cup. My mind was clear, and my intentions were known.

The cup floated up, the tea unmoving, and I focused my gaze to where I wanted it to go. Slowly, this time. Didn't want to have another episode like I had with the pillow last night. I let the cup drift toward Ryker and hover in front of him.

"I see someone has been practicing." He smiled as he took the cup that was suspended in mid-air, nodding his approval.

"Like I said, I couldn't sleep. Had the creepiest dream." I sat down opposite him with my own cup of tea. Having had too much coffee already, I needed to scale down a bit.

I told him about my dream. "There was a man, engulfed in flames and shrouded in darkness. He knew my name. Who I was. And there was a woman. She kept him away from me . . . She called him Gorice. I think what troubled me the most was that he looked just like you."

"That was no dream. You were astral projecting. What you saw was Gorice trying to reach you in the ethereal."

"How is that even possible?"

"Even though Gorice's soul is trapped in the ethereal, he still holds a lot of power."

"How did he get trapped there? And what is with the fire?" I asked, taking a bite from a cookie. Ryker did the same, seeming to contemplate what to say.

"Gorice is evil. I have told you that as I have told you that he wanted the power of the Pure. Kaye saw this happen before it came to pass. She had a connection to Gaia, the goddess of the earth, which allowed her to see her fate. When Kaye witnessed her own death, she knew what she had to do. Our daughter came early, as if she knew her life was in danger. Kaye cast the spell that would hide the bloodline until it was time.

"She also cast the spell to transfer her power to me upon her death. With a last goodbye, she sent Samena and me into hiding while she waited for Gorice. She knew he would come for us, and when he did, we would be safe. She did a spell so powerful that sent Gorice into the ethereal, but it also claimed her life. No one who had ever done such magic survived, and Kaye knew it. The spell was so strong that it deci-mated our cabin. There was nothing left."

Ryker grew quiet, probably thinking back to that time. Even I had tears running down my cheeks. I could see that he still loved her and that he missed her terribly. It must have been difficult to know what would happen without being able to do anything about it.

"I'm so sorry, Ryker," I whispered as I reached across the table to touch his arm.

He put his hand over mine, not saying a word.

"That would explain why you saw him in the fire. The cabin exploded with him inside." He'd put on his mentor mask, but I could still see the sadness haunting him.

"It doesn't explain why he looked like you. At first, I thought it was you, but the eyes were different, and he was shrouded in darkness. Why?"

"Well, now, there's a reason for that. The darkness changes a person. Your entire demeanor is affected. Even the eyes lose their light. As for the face . . ." He took a deep breath. "Gorice is my twin brother."

I gasped. I was not expecting that. I'd half expected the theory I had about not being able to dream about people you'd never seen. But Ryker had said it wasn't a dream, that it was astral projection.

"If he's your brother, how the hell did he become Tainted. How did you stay . . . you?" I asked, unable to wrap my head around the evil dude being his twin. Talk about cliché.

"I am not sure why my brother became Tainted. It could have had something to do with Kaye."

"What do you mean?" It seemed like everything involved Kaye.

"We all grew up together, before the world became what it is now. We were best friends, especially Gorice and I. We both fell in love with Kaye and have been in love with her since. She, however, chose me. I suspect it was the start of Gorice becoming Tainted. He wanted to prove that he was better than me. Stronger, more powerful. I never thought it would end like this."

I sat there and processed everything. It was a lot to take in. My oats had become cold, so I placed it in the microwave to heat it. I think that I needed something else to do, as I didn't have words for Ryker, and I didn't want to just sit there and stare at him.

The microwave pinged and I took my bowl out, then sat back down and started spooning the porridge into my mouth to avoid talking.

The revelation left an unpleasant taste in my mouth, which caused the food to taste terrible. I tried to swallow it down with my tea, but the taste still lingered. Like a story you thought was a joke that ended up being a true-life horror instead.

Ryker gazed at me, almost as if he was trying to read my thoughts. Every time I looked up, I caught him. Just sitting there, staring.

"What?" I asked with a mouthful of the foul-tasting oats.

"You seem to be taking this much better than your mom did."

"You never speak about her."

"Her passing is still so fresh in my memories, that I don't really want to think about it. Remember, I had four hundred years to deal with Kaye's death, and it still haunts me. Imagine how Samena's death is to me."

"Can I ask what happened to her? I remember you said that it was an accident, but considering what I know now . . ." I trailed off, hoping he'd fill in the blanks.

Ryker gave a sad sigh as he closed his eyes, recalling the past. "Your mother was a spirited woman. She had Kaye's tenacity, which I also see in you. Samena was wild and free, but when I told her how her mother passed, she wanted nothing to do with magic. She bound your powers, too, which is why it only showed up when your life was in danger." He took a deep breath, perhaps to collect his thoughts or to give me time to process.

"It was a winter's day. Snow covered the ground, and your mother thought that it would be a fun family outing to go skating on the lake. You were about two years old, if that. I took the toboggan with so that I could pull you along for a ride. It is one of my favorite days, but also Samena's last, which I suppose makes it my worst day, too.

"I taught you to make snowballs and persuaded you to throw it at your mother. You giggled so hard that you fell over, and a snowball fight ensued. For a while we were a real, normal family. Suddenly, your mother stopped and looked grim. She dropped the snowball, ran to grab you up into her arms, then rushed over to me, thrusting you at me. She told me to take you home, and to leave her there. I wanted to argue, to tell her she was being stupid, but the look in her eyes . . . Kaye had had that same look when she said goodbye to me." He rubbed his face as if to ease the emotions away.

"Samena kissed you on the cheek, telling you how much she loved you and that she would always be there for you. Then she kissed me and told me to protect you with my life. I begged her not to go, that I should be the one, but she cut me off."

I could see a knot forming in his throat, which made my own emotions stir up. This was so hard on him, losing his wife and his daughter, and feeling so utterly useless to do anything about it.

"She told me I was the only one who could protect you. That if she didn't do this, we would all die and Gorice would win. She hugged me, murmured that she loved us both, and then she took off toward the frozen lake. I held you tight, like I had your mother when she was a baby, and ran through the snow as fast as I could.

"After I buckled you in your car seat and closed the door, I looked over to your mother. She stood on the frozen lake, and ten figures surrounded her, stalking her like she was prey. She must have channeled her powers, the ones she'd sworn she would never use again. A blinding white light cascaded from the lake, engulfing everyone. When the light dissipated, not a soul was left in sight. I thought the water had claimed them, but a search came up with nothing. I packed our things, and we moved to a new state, changed our names and started anew. That is why I've always been so overprotective of you." When he looked me in the eyes, and it seemed as if Ryker had aged a couple of years just in those moments.

My heart wanted to break not only for him, but for me, for my mother, for the life we could have had, had it not been for the ridiculous notion of power created by some super dumbass.

I stood up and walked over to him, wrapping my arms around his shoulder for a hug. He returned the hug. I didn't know who needed the comfort more.

"What about my father? Do you know anything about him?"

Ryker looked at me for a while, as if contemplating telling me, but decided against it. "I think that is enough story time for one day. We have work to do. Since you have done so well harnessing your magic, I think today we shall train in the art of fighting."

And that was it. No explanation on my family tree or anything.

I wasn't going to push it . . . yet.

CHAPTER 9

I landed on my back with a hard thud. It was the hundredth time that I had bailed on my ass since we started this training program Ryker was so adamant on.

"Why the hell do we even have to do this?" I asked as I got to my feet and dusted off my clothes.

"Because, dear one, there will come a time when a place has been warded against magic, so your powers would be of absolute no use to you. You will need to know how to fight physically to protect yourself."

I understood his sentiment, but what the hell was he actually trying to teach me? That I was useless with hand to hand? That I couldn't seem to handle myself that well? That if I get attacked again, I would be absolutely useless without my powers? It pissed me off, and when Ryker invited me to attack him again, I used all the pent-up irritation and went in for the takedown.

But within a few seconds, I was back on the ground, staring up at the bright blue sky. The sky was mocking me, laughing its bright little ass off, trying to make me feel stupid and inferior.

"Seriously? How am I supposed to take you down? You're much

stronger than me and taller. This is useless." I threw up my hands in surrender as I stood up again.

"Ah, that's the predicament. Remember, every attacker you will ever come across will be bigger, stronger, and taller than you. No attacker will ever go easy on you just because you're a girl. No such luck. Now that you have learned that lesson, let me teach you the right way to do it."

He motioned for me to come closer again, walking me through a move if I ever had to take a guy to the ground—one arm around the attacker's waist, the other hand grabbing the leg closest to me. Once I lifted the leg, the attacker would be off balance and fall to the ground.

It was such a simple move that I thought there must have been something more to it. For the next few hours, Ryker taught me various tricks on takedowns, attacks, as well as basic weapon disarming. I knew there was a hell of a lot more to learn, but this would definitely help me get out of a situation if the need arose.

Ryker was about to teach me combination attacks with sticks as well as how to defend from those attacks when his phone rang on the porch. He ignored it, but when it rung a second time, he dropped the sticks and walked over to the table.

He picked up the phone, but I couldn't hear what he was saying. When he ended the call, he said, "That's all for today. I need to go. Feel free to practice some more if you like."

"Ryker? I was wondering if maybe I could go with Dakin and Mae to Newt's for a while. You know, catch up and all. I know it's only been a few days, but with everything that has happened . . . I just need a break?" I asked, hoping for the right answer.

He turned around, looked at me, then nodded. "Take your phone and call me immediately if you feel the slightest bit uncomfortable. Doesn't even matter if something just gives you the creeps. Call me."

I nodded my understanding, and he headed inside the house.

I stepped on to the porch and picked up my phone from the table. I sent out a broadcast message to Mae and Dakin, asking them if they wanted to join me at Newt's in thirty minutes.

As I went inside to take a shower, my phone pinged with messages of confirmation from my friends. I suddenly felt very nervous. I don't know why, though, they were my best friends. Maybe it was because I hadn't been able to process what had transpired over the last few days, so I wouldn't even know how to explain it to them if they asked.

Hell, I don't even know if I could tell them. Ryker hadn't told me whether I could. I hated these moral-compass dilemmas.

I got out of the shower, dressed, and was out of the door in a few minutes. The juice bar wasn't too far from my home, but my anxiety wouldn't settle. While walking through the streets, I kept looking around me, being as vigilant as Ryker had told me to be since I was a kid. But this time it was even more of a task knowing that people out there were actually after me.

When I got to the juice bar, I checked behind me one last time, but there was nothing out of the ordinary. No weird cars parked on the corner giving me the creeps, no people in dark clothing watching me. Nothing that would indicate that my life was in any danger.

The juice bar was crowded with people mulling around, talking. A stage with a sound system and a standing microphone had been erected against one wall. This must have been what Mae had been talking about when she said Newt wanted to upgrade the activities here.

I looked across the room and found Dakin sitting at a table at the far back. He waved me over with a huge smile on his face. His black hair seemed disheveled as if he was trying to go for a shorter version of a One Direction haircut. His bright blue eyes gleamed with excitement, and I knew he was bursting with something to tell us.

"It's so good to see you! How are you?" he asked when I sat down.

"Easy there, Hammy, I haven't even had my coffee yet." I grinned at him. No matter what mood I was in, being around Dakin always brightened my day.

"Sorry, I'm just happy to see you."

"I know. Who wouldn't be happy with me around?" I mocked as I waved the waiter over and ordered a caramel coffee shake. "What have you been up to?" I asked as the waiter left with our orders.

"Oh, the usual, you know. Part-time gig at the family business," he muttered nonchalantly, as if it was a given that he would be working there. His parents owned and worked at the local animal rescue and training center. It suited them, as the entire family portrayed empathy, patience, and love wherever they went.

"Any new, cute photos you can share?" Dakin always showed us the most adorable pics of the animals he worked with. Especially in the rescue center, which usually had abandoned babies. It always broke my heart when he told me what happened to them.

"Not today. It's mostly just been training, no new rescues to talk about. But enough about me. How you holding up? After the park, I mean?"

Was this going to be the new thing? Everyone asking me how I feel, how I'm doing? Whether I was coping?

"I'm alive, aren't I? So, I'd say I'm good."

He just nodded in agreement as the waiter came back with our drinks.

"Where's Mae?" I asked, glancing around.

"She'll be here soon, just running a bit late."

"On a totally different, less gloomy note. Do you think Newt's idea for karaoke nights will work?" I gestured to the stage.

"Could be fun. Maybe we should come one night. We can't do any worse than some people here already." He cocked his head toward a group of girls, adamantly flipping through a file filled with song titles. The group squealed with excitement as they found the song they were looking for. Dakin and I exchanged looks, and we both packed up with laughter. If their singing was anything like their squeals, the cat on a hot tin roof would seek cover tonight.

The door to Newt's chimed as someone entered. The blonde hair of my best friend bounced around as she tried to make her way around the group of people standing around. When she finally made it through, she nearly ran into me when our eyes met. She wrapped her arms around me in a tight hug. One would have thought we hadn't seen each other for months.

"I'm so happy you're okay," she mumbled against my shoulder as she squeezed me tighter. "I'm so, so sorry. I should have gone with you. I should have been there when they attacked and—"

"If you were there, then we both might have been in trouble," I whispered, rubbing her back to assure her that she had nothing to be sorry about. After a few seconds, which felt like minutes, she let me go and sat down, ordering her own drink.

"Okay, so now that I finally have you both here," Dakin started, and I could see the excitement he'd been holding back was about to come out. "I was thinking that maybe we should go to the lake next week? Just have some fun in the sun, splash around, have a picnic and just do what teenagers are supposed to do." Hope filled his eyes as he waited for us to make our decisions.

"I think that would be a great idea! Get some change of scenery," Mae replied, already getting her phone out to make a list of what we would need to take along.

"It would be fun, but I'd have to speak to Ryker first. After the attack, he's been even more protective than before. Which I understand now."

Dakin and Mae looked at each other as if conveying a message between them.

"I saw that. Spill," I said, wanting to know what that look was about. Mae's drink arrived, and she waited until the waiter was out of earshot before she spoke.

"Has Ryker started 'training' you yet?" The way she said 'training' made me think she knew something.

"What are you talking about? What training?" I asked, hoping that playing ignorant would make them drop the subject.

"You know what I'm talking about. We both know that you know what I'm talking about. Trust me, you can tell us."

I looked down at my shake, tracing some perspiration from my glass. I would draw on the table if it would mean avoiding their gazes and this conversation.

Silence descended upon our table. No one said anything. I wanted them to drop this entire conversation, but they were waiting for me to confess. I still didn't know if I could say anything. I didn't want to be the cause of a family secret to come out and bite both Ryker and me in the ass. We had enough to worry about.

I gazed around the room, looking for something or someone to save me from this moment. The squealing girls were sitting bunched up together, giggling about something on one of their phones. The D&D players were packed on the couches in the corner, immersed in their latest quest.

Everyone was caught up in their own conversations. No one was paying attention to a silent plea from an uncomfortable girl in the corner. Not even the waiters paid any attention to us. It was almost like we didn't exist.

"Amy." Mae took a deep breath, placing her hand on my arm to get my attention. "I know. Everything. The reason I know is that . . ." She looked around the room, making sure no one would overhear her. She lowered her voice to a whisper before she said the words that doused me with ice water.

"I'm a witch."

CHAPTER 10

Shock coursed through my body. Was I even breathing?

Had I heard her correctly? How had I not realized that my best friend was a magical being? Granted, a week ago I didn't even believe in anything that couldn't be explained with factual evidence.

Dakin giggled. "I think you broke her."

"I did not break her, she just needs to process," Mae retorted, then turned back to me and said in a gentle voice, "Amy? Honey, are you okay?"

"Does she look okay? Maybe we need some water," Dakin said sarcastically.

"She still has a shake. Why would she need water?"

"Not to drink, blondie, to throw in her face so she can snap out of it."

"I'm not throwing her with water. Are you mad?"

"Well, then, you'll have to wait until she pulls herself back to herself.
"

"Listen here, mister—"

"Can you guys stop bickering? I'm processing over here!"

Their eyes darted toward me, their minor squabble immediately forgotten.

"Finally! She awakes." Dakin laughed while Mae just rolled her eyes at him.

Just as Mae opened her mouth to start speaking, I held up my hand and took a long sip of my shake, hoping that the cold and the caffeine would wake up my brain.

"How did I never know? Why didn't you ever tell me?" I asked.

"Would you have believed me if I had told you? You were a skeptic all your life. You probably would have thought I was yanking your chain."

"True, but still, you could have given hints, or eased me into it or something."

"Really? You never wondered why I had an intense knowledge of the arcane?"

"I did, but I always just brushed it off as you being a fan of the occult."

Mae laughed, but it was cut short with a snort from Dakin. I could see in his eyes that he wanted to make some smart-ass reply.

"Do I look like an occult groupie?" she asked, brushing her perfectly styled blonde hair off her shoulders. Her chocolate brown eyes dared me to say yes, but the lack of any piercings or mystical tattoos said otherwise. Except for the small arrow tattooed on her wrist, which she explained was a reminder to always walk her own path, she looked like the normal fashionista teenager everyone always looked to for the latest trends.

"Not at all, Mae. I didn't mean it like that."

"Oh hush, you know I'm just messing with you." She smiled, waving me off as she took a sip of her Very Berry smoothie.

"Well, at least you now know what goes on behind closed doors with her. To some extent," Dakin teased, arching his eyebrows suggestively.

"Well, at least I've come clean now, haven't I?" Mae chimed, and to the normal ears one would think it was a normal banter, but I sensed an underlining secret that they hadn't shared with me yet.

"When did this happen?" I asked. I knew I sounded like a newb, but in my defense, I totally was.

"Some people make it happen later in life, but I was born this way."

"Thank you, Lady Gaga."

Mae gave Dakin the evil eye but ignored his comment and carried on with her explanation.

"As I was saying before I was so rudely interrupted. My magic came with a lifetime of studying and training. I wasn't born with the natural *je ne sais quoi* like you, meaning that I can't just make things happen, I have to prepare for it. No matter how trained I am, witches still need the spells. So, my training will never end, but I will always live in the light."

I soaked up her words, trying to unravel them in my mind. "How do you know about me?"

"Everyone knows about you. Well, in the magical community, at least," Dakin responded, looking half-bored with the conversation.

"What my esteemed idiot wanted to say is that everyone in the magical community knows about the Pures. It's like an urban legend in our world. On the note of how I knew it was you . . ." Mae thought about the answer for a while, taking small sips from her smoothie. "I was doing a scrying spell, looking for a source of power powerful enough. We had felt a stir in the energies, something strong but dark. A danger was coming, and we feared we wouldn't be strong enough to defeat it."

"Wait, who is 'we?'" I asked.

"We, as in the coven I'm in."

"Oh, right. Of course."

"Anyway, every time I scried for a power source strong enough to defeat the impending danger, it always pointed to you. Thought it was a fluke, that maybe the pendulum was picking up a ley-line or something. The thing is, whenever you moved, it moved."

"Okay, but it still doesn't really explain how you know about me. Did Ryker say something?"

Dakin and Mae again shared a glance, which confirmed that they were holding out on me.

"Ryker caught me doing the spell at the shop. Asked me what I was looking for, so I came clean. He told me to stop looking, that it wasn't safe. That lives would be in danger. That your life would be in danger.

He told me you are the last Pure and that the danger we were all sensing is the Tainted coming to claim what they wanted."

"Wow. So, Ryker told you, but I had to find out when I was attacked. Like what am I, chopped liver?" I was glad that Mae told me, but I was pretty pissed that Ryker had said nothing to me. "You're a witch, too? Or mage, or whatever the term is for male witches." I glared at Dakin, daring him to prove me wrong.

"Actually no. I'm a familiar."

"Like a witch's cat? But you're human."

"Technically, yes, like a witch's cat, but different. We are there to guide new beings to the light and help them harness their magic. I am human because I haven't received my shape yet."

"What's your excuse for not saying anything?" I snapped.

"Well, by our rules, we are not allowed to say anything until our charges come into power."

"Then why are you telling me this now?" I folded my arms across my chest.

Dakin looked at me with a raised eyebrow, waiting for the pieces to click into place in my mind.

"Oh! Wait, I'm your charge?" I asked, surprised and flattered that the universe would think I needed a familiar.

"Yes. I couldn't say anything to you until you had powered up."

"Okay, I get it. Both of you. I understand, but don't think I'm not peeved about being left out of the loop." But my irritation dissipated with every second that ticked by.

We spent the rest of the afternoon joking around and planning our trip to the lake. If Ryker would allow me to go. We even tried to think of ways to convince him to let me go.

My phone pinged with a text, and when I checked, I saw it was Ryker asking me where I was. Rolling my eyes, I texted back that I was at the juice bar with Dakin and Mae, exactly where I'd told him I'd be.

My phone rang, and Ryker's name flashed on the screen.

With a huff, I answered.

"Amunet! You need to get home, now!"

"Ryker, what's going on? I told you—"

"Now, Amunet! Something has happened." The urgency in his tone made my blood run cold. I couldn't remember him ever speaking to me with such impatience. Something was definitely up.

"I'm on my way." I disconnected the call and looked at my friends. "I'm sorry, but Ryker needs me to go home. Now."

"I'll drop you off," Dakin said as he stood up. We settled our bill and headed toward Dakin's pickup truck around the corner. It was a red, older model Ford, which he usually used when he was working at the rescue center.

Dakin unlocked the truck and started the engine while clipping in his seatbelt. My mind raced with various scenarios of what could have happened to make Ryker so impatient and desperate.

"Why do you think Ryker wants you home?" Dakin asked, glancing at me as we turned onto my street.

"I don't know. I was literally just wondering the same thing."

He pulled up in front of my house. "Whatever it is, you know you got me if you need to talk."

"Thanks, Dakin. For everything."

He smiled as I got out of the car.

The lights were on, and I could see movement inside. My stomach turned as I marched up the walkway to the front door. The door opened before I could grip the handle. Ryker stood there, worry in his eyes. I turned around and waved at Dakin, letting him know I was okay now. As I stepped into the house, he drove off.

"Ryker? What's wrong?" I asked, setting my things down by the door and moved past him as he closed the door behind me. He motioned to the living room, and I followed.

"There have been some . . . developments. We'll need to increase your training, and it's time for you to learn the more difficult things—disarming people with weapons, how to fight with those weapons and the harder spells."

"Why? I mean, I know we were eventually moving toward these

things, but why now? Why the urgency?" I sat back in my chair, crossing my legs as I made myself comfortable.

"The call I received earlier today was from an old acquaintance who has kept me up to speed on all things magical beyond our borders. He called to tell me that there were rumors that a Tainted could possess a human."

"I thought only things like demons could do something like that."

"That is usually the case, yes, but there have been stories that if someone was powerful enough, they could possess a person, taking over their bodies for a period of time." Ryker clasped his hands together as he rested his elbows on his knees, looking weary.

"Okay . . . So, what? I'm going to train on how to depossess these humans like in *The Exorcist*?"

"I see you have been peeking at the advanced magic. In a way, yes. You'd learn that, but also how to deal with anything in that situation. You see, the Tainted the rumors are about is Gorice." His statement made me sit upright, tension shooting into my shoulders, my mind reeling.

"Wait? He's here? I mean, I dreamed about it, and when I woke up, I had a gut feeling that he was close, but I thought it was only because of the dream. How is it even possible? I thought you said he's in the ethereal?" Knowing that Gorice was capable of such feats made my stomach tighten.

"He is, but remember, before Gorice died, he claimed the power of many Pures. Some of that could have left residue, which he has now learned to harness. That could be why he has been able to possess vessels for a time being."

"What does that mean for us? For me?"

"It would mean that we have our work cut out for us. He hasn't learned how to harness his vessel's powers yet, but that doesn't mean it won't happen. It would also mean that we do not know who he is, so we cannot trust anyone."

CHAPTER 11

Over the next week, Ryker completely shed his calm mentoring demeanor and took on the role of sadistic drill sergeant. The work we'd been doing had been a thousand times worse than what I'd thought was tough.

Every morning started the same, with a couple of miles' worth of jogging for him and me, and me complaining that I was not a runner. I joked that if I was running like that, it would be because someone was chasing m. That comment cost me fifty burpees.

By the end of that exercise, I felt like puking. Did we stop? Hell no, that was only the warm-up according to Ryker. We did strength training, cardio, bootcamp, and Krav Maga—the military self-defense tactic to disarm your opponent and make them submit. That was the only physical training I enjoyed.

Even though these training regimes were supposed to strengthen me, I'd never felt this weak in my life. By lunch, I was exhausted. My body ached in places I hadn't even thought was possible.

We didn't stop after lunch. That was when the mental exercises came into play.

Ryker would call for something, and I would have to respond with the spell—saying the spell and performing the magic. He'd light a fire, and I would have to manipulate it into whatever he wanted or use one of the other elements to douse it. Water to drown the flames or wind to smother it. The combinations were extreme but effective.

"Now, I want you to become invisible. I don't want to see a shimmer out of place." He motioned at my body, waiting for me to do the spell and complete the transformation. I closed my eyes, my mental and physical fatigue overwhelming me.

"Bright light, dark night. Cloak me in light as dark as night," I whispered, waiting for the magic to take hold and cloak me. The tingling heat traveled through my body as the power in me took hold. To myself, I looked normal, but when I looked at Ryker, his face was expressionless, but the look in his eyes gave way to pride.

"And what about the spell to make the invisible seen?"

"*Aspectus Invisus.*" My cloak drained from me, revealing my position but also revealing a chest sitting on the ground next to Ryker.

"How long has that been there?" I asked, eyeing the chest suspiciously.

"The entire time we were training. I hid it outside and cloaked it before our run this morning. That is another thing you would need to practice. To see the things that are hidden from sight."

"I could just perform the spell."

"But what if you were surrounded by humans and couldn't reveal something without giving yourself away? Or what if you were on a recon mission, looking for something that a host kept secret for a reason?"

"Okay, Doctor Strange. I get it. How do I see past the spell?"

"First, you will need to feel for the magic. This might take some practice, so close your eyes." He came to stand next to me. "Now, hold out your hands, palms facing down. Feel the energy coursing through the earth."

I did as he asked. I could feel my magic stirring. I set my intentions on feeling the energy of earth. I could hear Ryker walk around me as he spoke.

"What do you see?"

"I can feel the vibrations. The colors I keep seeing are black and green."

"Good. The green is nature, the black is the grounding spirit of the earth. Some even see it as an obsidian crystal and use it to ground themselves. Now, try to expand the vibrational energy. Everything and everyone gives it off. You will soon get to the point where you will identify someone by the vibe they give off."

I tried expanding the view of energy to incorporate other things and other beings. I could see the animals and insects in the ground, the inanimate objects around the yard.

"Your energy is blue," I told Ryker. I could feel and see him walking around me. I felt like Daredevil being able to see without my eyes. This definitely had some benefits.

"Very good. What else do you see?"

I told him about the rest of the things until I picked up on an energy that seemed to sparkle. Like trying to look in a broken mirror. I could see the vibrations, but I could also sense that something was trying to hide it. I opened my eyes and looked in the direction where I could feel the pulsing.

At first, I couldn't see anything, but I knew something was there. I could feel it. I stared at the spot so intently that I swore I was going mad, but then I saw a shimmer run across an invisible object.

"There." I pointed. I walked over and repeated the spell to make the invisible seen. The chest that had been next to Ryker materialized.

Was this another one?

I looked back at the first one, and being zoned in on the illusion magic of invisibility, I noticed the chest looked wrong. It shimmered, even though it had already been revealed. Something was definitely up with it.

I walked over to the illusion and tried to think of which spell would work best. I could use the truth spell, or I could try the hidden one that would show me what was hidden beneath this shimmer. Or the return spell that could return it to its former state.

"*Reverte!*" I said as I spoke the spell to return it to its former state. The magic responded, and the spell faded away, revealing a cookbook. I picked it up and showed it to Ryker.

"Wonderful!" He clapped his hands together, taking the book from me. "I was wondering if you would be able to figure it out."

"So, what's next?"

"Next, we will discuss the powerful spells, now that you can identify magic and track its energies."

He spoke about the things that every magic user should always remember. To never do magic with negativity. It would always backfire and bite you in the ass. He told me about when to use magic and when to use illusions.

We discussed the various scenarios in which that would happen, and he even laid out the spells in the grimoire and when to use them and how.

By the end of the day, my mind overflowed with information. My body was exhausted, and my head was trying to make sense of everything. It was hard to imagine that only a few weeks ago I had been oblivious to all of this and now I could do amazing things with my magic.

I fell asleep, contemplating the differences between what I could do and what other magic users could do.

When I woke the next morning, it felt like a freight train had hit me. My body screamed at me for the torture it had endured. My head felt thick with exhaustion, and I knew I wouldn't be able to do anything Ryker set out for me today.

I got up and dressed, my body protesting every movement. This was going to be a long-ass day.

Without a word to Ryker, I headed out the door and made my way to the bookstore. I stopped at Newt's and grabbed coffee for myself and Mae before I headed to the store.

As I opened the door to *WordCraft*, the small bell above the door chimed.

Mae glanced at me from behind the counter. She was busy with a customer, an old lady looking for something specific, so I waved at Mae and headed to the lounge area to wait. Knowing full well that the older generation could be tedious clientele, I made myself comfortable on the small sofa and took a sip of my coffee.

On the small coffee table next to the couch, I noticed an array of strange books that hadn't been put away yet. One book caught my attention as it peeked out underneath the stack beside me. I set my coffee down and lifted the stack to pull it out.

Placing the book on my lap as I set the rest down again, I noticed it was a hardcover, bound in a reddish-brown color with gold lettering embossed on the cover. I read the title. It was a book about possession.

From what I gathered from the headings and paging through it, the book helped you tell if someone was possessed and what to do about it. The section of tell-tale signs caught my attention, and I decided to read more about that.

The most obvious signs of possession was the change in eye color, a change in demeanor and how they usually did things. A possessed person's body language would differ from how they usually carried themselves, and their voice would change in tone and vibrations.

I heard the chime from the door as the old lady left the store, but I only looked up when Mae joined me.

"Doing some light reading?"

I laughed at the silliness of it all as I placed the book back on the stacks and handed Mae her cup of coffee.

"So, what's up with the book?"

"Oh, it was just here on the table. You'll think it's weird, but Ryker told me about this guy from the past who has the ability to possess people. That he could be anyone at any time. So, when this book peeked out from underneath the stack . . . I just thought it was more than just coincidence, you know?" I took a sip from my coffee, waiting for Mae to talk smack and mock me on my choice of literature, but she surprised me.

"Gorice. I heard about that." Mae nodded in understanding as she took a sip from her own drink.

"How do you know about it? How do you know about Gorice?"

"It's a long story. One that you will definitely hate me for."

"I will never hate you. I might be mad, sure, but hate? Never."

Mae took a few more sips of her coffee, as if contemplating her words and trying to figure a way out of it.

I mimicked her drinking and raised my eyebrow expectantly.

"Okay, fine. Stop staring at me like that," she started. "Just remember, you asked for this. We have been friends for what, five years now?" Mae looked at me for confirmation, and I just nodded, not wanting to derail her speech.

"All I have ever wanted was to be your friend. To watch out for you and keep you safe. I never thought that it would ever go this far, but I can't turn back the hands of time now." Her words made my stomach flip. I had a bad feeling that she hadn't just heard about Gorice through research.

"It was about three years ago. Ryker came to see my mom. She is the High Priestess of the local coven. He told her that dark times are looming ahead, and that he needed eyes and ears around town, especially around you. He told my mother about Gorice and the ascending dangers of the Tainted. He said that it would be in everyone's best interest if he knew what you were doing, who you were speaking to, and any 'odd' occurrences that happened that might put you in danger."

I wanted to speak up and tell her it's all good, but Mae cut me off with a gesture of her hands.

"If I don't tell you everything now, I might never get the courage to do so again. Ryker had this sixth sense that something would happen. He didn't know when, but he said he felt it in his bones. Naturally, my mother agreed that it would be for the best to be on the lookout for anything and to keep you safe. Because you and I were already friends, I was called upon to be their eyes and ears around you and to report anything out of the ordinary to them."

Shock smashed through me as the truth left Mae's lips. A range of emotions wrestled inside me, and I didn't know which one was stronger. The lies, the betrayal, the secrets. It all came tumbling down around me.

"I'm such an idiot," I whispered, jerking to my feet. How could I have never known? How could Ryker have done this to me? I felt like I was living with a fake sense of individuality.

"Amy, please. Sit down so that we can talk."

"Talk? You want to talk now? You could have told me this a long time ago!"

"I wanted to, believe me, I did. But because you didn't know about who you were destined to be, everything had to be kept a secret."

"So, if my powers never manifested, I would never have known about this? About how you and Ryker lied to me? How you betrayed my trust and made me think you were my friend?" I rushed to the door when Mae grabbed my arm and turned me around.

"We *are* friends! Look, I'm sorry for—"

I cut her off as my rage took control of me. "Sorry? What are you sorry for? For lying to me through our entire friendship? For keeping life-changing secrets from me? For conspiring with Ryker behind my back for years? For spying on me?" Red filled my vision. The only thing I saw now wasn't my best friend who had helped me through a lot, but rather a traitor. An enemy to what I had once held dear.

"A best friend is supposed to be someone you trust, and right now I can't trust anyone!" My magic caught on my anger, and as I got everything off my chest, the shelves started shaking, pitching rows and rows of books to the ground.

With shock on her face, Mae let go of my arm and turned to see the books tumbling to the ground and her powerless to stop it. I used that opportunity to walk through the door and leave the conversation behind.

Next stop on my rage train was Ryker.

I slammed the front door shut behind me. My anger seethed through my veins like drugs through an addict. Storming through the house, I found Ryker in the kitchen, preparing lunch.

"What the fuck is wrong with you?!"

The smile on his face vanished as I stalked closer to him. "It's one thing to keep secrets from me, which I now understand and can even look past, but what gave you the right to think that it was okay to use my best friend to spy on me?" My magic was feeding on my anger, but I couldn't care less.

"Amunet, calm—"

"You don't get to tell me to calm down! You have been in control of my life the entire time! Did you really think I wouldn't find out? That I wouldn't have a shit fit about being lied to, manipulated, and betrayed?"

"Amunet, if you would just listen—"

"I am done listening! This has gone on far too long. I'm tired of being used. I'm tired of being manipulated and treated like a child. I'm beyond tired of all the lies and secrets that you hold back from me." As I kept yelling at Ryker, my power ignited. The kitchen appliances started floating around the room. The chairs were bumping against the table, trying to get out of their places.

I wanted to scream. To cry and break things. I wanted to explode with frustration and anger. My vision blurred like it had in the park when my magic manifested, but this time it wasn't from fear, it was from white, fiery rage. Ryker was talking to me, but I didn't want to hear a word that was coming out of his mouth.

The searing heat of my magic engulfed me, and I knew I wouldn't be able to rein it back in. Ryker must have known this because he grabbed hold of my face. He was talking to me again, but this time it wasn't that I didn't want to hear him. I couldn't hear his words over the hum of power. Ryker's hands on my face felt like dry ice. His lips were still moving as my vision went darker. The last thing I saw was Ryker hovering above me as my body made contact with the floor.

~

*I*t was dark when I finally came to. I looked around and saw Ryker sitting in his armchair, reading a book and drinking his tea. He noticed me staring at him and set the book down on his lap.

"Good, you're awake." He took a sip of his tea as I tried to sit upright. My head was pounding again, and I wished that just once, I would wake up on the sofa without a migraine.

"What happened?"

"Well, from what I can gather, your emotions sent your magic into overdrive, which basically caused you to become a superpowered nuke. I had to use a sleeping spell on you otherwise you might have exploded."

"Thanks." I lay back down, waiting for the throbbing pain to subside. "How does going nuke even happen?"

"I'm not entirely sure. I've never really experienced it in my four hundred years, but my theory is that if you channel your magic when your emotions are in twelfth gear, you start losing control. That's when things go wrong."

It made sense, in a way. It was hard enough to get control of my magic and some days harder to get a grip on my emotions. So, it was understandable that when both were out of whack, something terrible could happen.

I wanted to sit upright, but I winced when the hammer in my brain acted up again. Ryker looked at me and went to the kitchen. I could hear him opening cupboards, rustling cutlery together, and the kettle boiling.

Ryker came back with a cup of tea and a small plate with a sandwich on it. He handed me the plate and set the cup on the table in front of me. Taking the first bite of the bread, my stomach groaned with pleasure. I ate the first half of the delicious ensemble before sipping on the tea. I still didn't know how he did it, but Ryker always knew the perfect tea for any ailment.

"What had you in such a spin?" he asked as I took a bite of the next half of the sandwich.

I thought about his question a bit, taking another bite to focus my thoughts and weave them into words. After taking another sip of the tea, I told Ryker what had happened at the bookstore.

I felt betrayed, not only by Mae for keeping the secret but also by him for thinking it was a good idea to have my best friend spy on me all these years.

As I let everything out, tears blurred my vision, and I lost my appetite. The knot in my stomach came loose, and with it came a wave of nausea that threatened to expel the contents of my stomach.

All the hurt, lies, and betrayal hit me at once. It felt like I had suffered a significant loss I couldn't get back. Even thinking it made me feel stupid since none of the people had intended to hurt me, and Mae wasn't gone . . . but I knew deep down that it would take a long time before I would be ready to forgive her.

Ryker sat on the edge of his seat, running his hands through his brown salt-and-pepper hair. Sighing in exasperation, he looked at me, regret and sadness marring his face.

"What Mae told you was correct. But before you flip your sorceress switch again, let me explain. A lot of things were happening at the time. You were already showing signs of your magic. Though, it was little things, like being more empathetic and clair-cognitive, I knew it was only time before you would come into your full power.

"There were also talks amongst the magical community about a major power surge happening. No one knew why or even what it was, but we all felt it. At first, I thought you had finally ascended into your power, but when you came home that day and were still the person you were, I knew it was something else. Mae was already investigating it, and that's when I found her scrying. She tried to play it off as nothing, but I told her the infinite power she was searching for was closer than she thought. I knew that the Tainted would feel the power, too, and that one day they would come for you. You didn't stand a chance, then." Ryker sat there in silence, staring at a spot on the floor for a while.

"Is that why you asked Mae to spy on me?" I could feel my anger bubbling to the surface again. Taking a sip of the tea, I tried pushing it down.

Ryker nodded. "It wasn't spying. I was fearful that the Tainted would take you away from me, like they did your mother. Like they did Kaye. I only asked her to watch out for you and to keep you safe."

"That's what Mae said," I replied, then took a deep breath and let it out. "But how am I supposed to trust anyone, if everyone around me keeps lying and keeping secrets?"

"Amunet," Ryker started as he came to sit next to me. "The people in your life love you and only want what's best for you. I know what you are feeling right now is painful and that you feel that everyone in your life has done you wrong. That was never our intention at all. Just know that the ones who are here are the ones you can trust at all times." Ryker pulled me toward him as he wrapped his arms around me, rubbing my back in a supportive way, like he used to do when I was a kid.

"Remember one thing. You can trust anyone, but it's the devil inside them you cannot trust."

CHAPTER 13

"Ryker?" I asked the next morning when I sat down for breakfast. The events from the previous night still hung in the air. The shame of my reaction was a bigger weight than the betrayal.

Ryker looked up from the pan where he was flipping pancakes.

"I was wondering . . . Dakin planned a day out by the lake tomorrow and asked if I can go. Can I?" I let the question hang in the air. In a way, I hoped he would say no, but the other half of me thought it would be a great to get a break from everything that has happened in the last few weeks.

The silence was palpable, and I waited for him to say that it would be too dangerous. But when he placed a stack of pancakes in front of me, his words nearly sent me falling from the chair.

"I'm not fond of the idea, but I can't keep you captive with me forever. I also think that it might be a good idea for you to unwind and be a teenager for a bit."

"You serious?"

Ryker nodded, a smirk playing at the edges of his mouth. I was so relieved and excited that I jumped up from my chair and wrapped my arms around his shoulders, hindering the bite he was about to take. "Thank you!"

"I do have conditions, though."

"Of course, you do." I rolled my eyes playfully as I sat down and started digging into the breakfast.

"You can go, but I drop you off and pick you up."

"Wouldn't have it any other way."

We ate the stack of pancakes, making small talk about the lake and what Ryker would get up to when I was gone.

"I will enjoy the silence. Perhaps I'll take a nice, long bubble bath and read *Fifty Shades*," he joked.

"Just keep the shower head above water, please," I teased, knowing full well that he had no idea what the book was about.

"Why?"

"You don't know how raunchy those books are, do you?"

"That bad, huh?"

"I've never read it, couldn't get past the first chapter, but from what others have told me . . . let's just say that's why middle-aged women enjoy it."

He bursts out laughing, and the laugh was so contagious that I couldn't help joining in.

"Okay, I'll stick to my usual reads, then." He chuckled after our hysterics died down.

We cleaned up after breakfast, and Ryker told me to go with him to the bookstore. I was reluctant to go as I didn't want to face Mae at all, but Ryker just mentioned that while he was doing what he had to do, I could go to the store and get what I needed for the picnic. I agreed, and we left the house, still making jokes.

When Ryker parked the car outside his bookstore, I sat there for a while, just staring at the place, knowing that somewhere inside Mae would be busy working on something. She absolutely loved her job.

Ryker cleared his throat, then gave me a list of things he needed from the convenience store down the road. Handing over his credit card, he basically shoved me out of the vehicle.

~

*A*bout thirty minutes later, I walked out the store with two bags of groceries—things for the house and things I would need for the lake. The more I thought about the lake escapade, the more excited and nervous I became.

As I walked down the street toward the bookshop, so I could pack everything in the car, I saw Mae heading out of the bookstore. I ducked into the closest store I could find. I wasn't ready to face her yet. I was still upset about the secrets and ashamed about my behavior—even though it was completely justified. I knew that I would face her soon. I missed my best friend already, so maybe tomorrow would be the day, but right now I wasn't ready.

The store happened to be a clothing store. Rows and rows of clothes for every occasion hung around, just waiting for the right person to pluck them from their morbid spaces and give the item new life.

Perhaps while I was here, I would get a new swimsuit. I walked past the corporate wear. Thank goodness I didn't have to wear such stiff and unhappy clothes. The next rows were lined with summer apparel—long and short flowing dresses, crop tops, denim shorts, and everything else in between.

All the way at the back of the store, next to the underwear and pajamas, was an entire selection of swimwear ready to be inspected. Excitement rose within as the thought of getting something new stood mere feet away from me.

I inspected the racks. One pieces, bikinis, those that didn't know if they were full or bikini with the sides hollowed out, all hung there waiting to be chosen. If it wasn't difficult enough to make a choice based on the selection, the color schemes made it more difficult. Did I want something black or some color? Did I want something with a shimmer and patterns or a collage of various colors? Did I want something plain or something with a bit of a flair?

I'd definitely be busy here for a while.

"Amy?" While contemplating my choices, a voice sounded behind me. Turning to look, relief filled me when I saw my art teacher standing there with a few things draped over her arm. "What are you doing here?"

"Mrs. Wonder! I'm surprised to see you here. I'm just doing some window shopping for the lake tomorrow."

"Oh, wonderful! That should be a fun day out. I'm also updating my summer wardrobe a bit." Silence fell between us. Usually, it was comforting to talk to her, but now it seemed weird, what with her being Mae's mother and all. To avoid eye contact, I glanced at the swimwear again, rifling through the rows as if looking for a specific size.

"Amunet, are you sure you're all right?" She touched my shoulders and our eyes met. Her blue eyes were shaded with knowing as small wisps of hair curled around the corner of her eyes. She tilted her head slightly to the side in that unique way she had to show concern.

"Yes, everything is fine. Why do you ask?"

"You know the definition of fine, right? Freaking out, Insecure, Neurotic, and Emotional."

I laughed out loud at her attempt to be cool. "Where on earth did you hear that?"

"Oh, it's an old Aerosmith song, long before your time. But now, really? Are you sure you're not just hiding from something else?" She gestured to the window.

My gaze followed, and I saw Mae walking back to the bookstore. When I turned back to Mrs. Wonder, her eyes lit up, and I knew it was futile to try to hide anything from her.

"You heard about that?"

"My dear, there's very little that happens around here that I don't know about." She gave a hearty laugh, then she lowered her voice so only I could hear her. "Perks of being the High Priestess of the coven, don't you think?" She winked at me, and I gaped at her. Mae and Ryker had both mentioned this to me, but I hadn't thought she'd be so open about it with me.

I nodded. "I guess so."

What else was I supposed to do? This woman was like a mentalist.

She could see through everything and everyone. No one could hide secrets from her or even attempt to lie to her. She always knew. She placed her hand on my shoulders again as she pulled me in for a sideways hug.

"Sweetie, you should let it go and forgive. All these negative emotions are clouding your aura and messing with your magic. We can't have a powerful being such as yourself try to save the world when all is not right in here." She pressed a hand on my chest, just over my heart. I knew what she was saying was the truth. I needed to let go of everything that was troubling me.

Brushing a kiss on my head, she said goodbye and went to pay. A minute later, she waved at me as she left the store.

I stood in the swimwear section of the store, not really in the mood for shopping anymore. Mrs. Wonder's words bounced around my head like a tennis match between my thoughts.

Deciding that nothing would get me to enjoy shopping, I left the clothing store and walked down the sidewalk to the bookstore. Ryker was coming out of the store with one of the customers, laughing at something the elderly woman was saying.

"All right, Mrs. Brown, Mae or I will let you know when your order has come in. Shouldn't take more than a few days."

"Oh, thank you, young man." The old lady patted Ryker on the cheek, adjusted her purse hanging on her arm, and strode off toward her car. Ryker came toward me, still chuckling, and grabbed one of the bags from my hands.

"Ready to go?" he asked as he opened the trunk of the car and placed the groceries inside.

"Yeah, sure." I got into the car, still pondering Mrs. Wonder's words. I wouldn't be getting much sleep that night.

CHAPTER 14

The parking area at the lake came into view as we drove up. Cars and vans filled the parking area. Trees lined the sidewalk, which you had to walk past to get to the lake.

Ryker parked close to the tree line and switched off the car. After scanning the surroundings, he turned and looked at me. "Remember, things aren't always what they seem. Call me if anything, and I mean *anything*, feels off."

"I will, I promise." I started opening the door to get out.

"Amunet, wait."

I turned back, my hand resting on the door handle.

"I have something for you. It was Kaye's. It will offer protection when you need it." He held up a beautiful crescent moon dangling from a silver chain. The moon held a small amethyst at the top of its crescent, almost as if the crystal was its sun. The moon itself was endowed with stunningly intricate Celtic knots. I wanted to touch it, but I hesitated. I could feel the energy emanating from it.

"Kaye once told me the goddess Gaia herself had bestowed this charm upon her as a way to protect her in both the spiritual and earthly realms. It holds the connection to the ethereal, to the goddess herself," he said as he motioned for me to turn around so he could fasten it around my neck.

"Ryker, this is gorgeous. Thank you. I won't take it off."

"I just hope it will serve you as well as it served Kaye."

The charm brushed my collarbone as I leaned over to hug Ryker. When I pulled away, tears shimmered in Ryker's eyes, and my throat constricted with emotion.

"I'll call when I'm ready to go home." I opened the door, then left without another glance at him.

The car started, but I only looked back and waved when he had already driven off, knowing it would be too late for Ryker to notice it. I took a deep breath to settle myself, then walked through the dense trees toward the water.

River sand covered most of the walk to the lake. People already occupied the grass to my left. Families having a fun-filled day out were setting up the barbeques, the children running around and playing while the adults set the picnic benches. Boats and jet-skis were making waves deep in the water.

I spotted Dakin a few feet to my right, already setting up the picnic. I walked over to him and held out the cooler Ryker had persuaded me to bring.

"Someone called for some snacks?" I asked, indicating to the food inside the cooler.

"Finally! What took you so long?" Dakin mocked with a smile as he took the cooler from me and wrapped me in a one-armed hug.

"Oh, you know . . . this radiance doesn't come easy." I waved my hands down my body with a grin.

Dakin took one look at me and burst out laughing. "If this is you trying, then I don't want to know what you look like as a slouch."

I slapped him with the back of my hand in feigned offence. I was already having fun, and I just got here. But then again, Dakin could make anything fun—it's what he was good at. I helped Dakin finish setting up, but I kept looking toward the trees for the missing person in our trio. No sign of her, though.

"Where's Mae?"

"Oh, um . . . she canceled this morning. She didn't know if you wanted to see her, so she would rather not be the cause of an atmosphere."

"You heard about that?" I asked, pretending to hand iron wrinkles out of the blanket. Dakin nodded, and I could feel his eyes on me.

"To be honest, I don't blame you. I probably would have reacted the same if I was in your shoes. Well, minus the magic burst, though. It took Mae three hours to clean up the mess after you left the bookshop." Knowing that even Dakin thought my actions were justified didn't make me feel better about it. I felt even worse knowing that the books had taken so long to be set to rights. What type of friend destroys a store and leaves it for her best friend to sort out?

"Okay, enough wallowing. We're here to have fun, aren't we?" Dakin asked, handing me a cold soda from the cooler.

I nodded and accepted the drink. Sitting down in a comfortable position, I could scope out the shoreline. Fires had been started, and woodsmoke wafted through the air. Kids were playing and splashing around. Some people had even brought their canine friends who were enjoying the water more than the kids. Boats roared on the water, tugging along tubes and other inflatables, throwing unexpecting riders to the water on tight turns. A smile spread across my face. This was the life.

"Are we gonna soak up the sun all day or are we going swimming?" Dakin asked as he pulled off his shirt and stepped out of his shoes simultaneously. Even though Dakin and I had been friends since elementary school and I saw him as my annoying brother, I couldn't help but admire his physique.

Since he'd started working at the rescue center in junior high, Dakin had become more confident, more built. And for the first time, I actually took notice.

"Amy? You got a little drool right here," Dakin said, pulling me out of my trance. He indicated the side of his mouth where the imaginary drool was.

I glared at him and shot to my feet, chasing him, but he was fast. I quickly stripped down to my swimsuit, then ran after him into the water.

Even though the sun was already blistering hot this time of day, the water was chilled enough to counteract the heat. I swam toward Dakin, and when I grabbed him, I put all my weight on his shoulders, dunking him under the water. I had won that round.

I eased up on the dunking and drifted on my own, only to be grabbed by my feet and pulled under as well. The chill of the water was a shock to my face, but the relief from the sun felt glorious. I came up for air and rubbed the excess water from my face. Dakin was swimming around me, waiting for me to surface.

"Bitch." I splashed water into his face.

He immediately counteracted with the famous *Supernatural* comeback we'd been using since we binge-watched the show. "Jerk."

Goofing off felt so good that all my worries and stress was forgotten, and I felt like a regular teenager again, just hanging out with one of my best friends. It would have been better if Mae was there, though. Just the thought of her made my mood drop, but before I could give in to the emotion, Dakin gave another challenge.

"How about a race?"

"A race? Really?"

"Yeah, why not? Say, to the floating pier? If I win, we go out on one of the rowboats?"

"And if I win?" I asked him, quirking one eyebrow.

"That will never happen. But if you win, I'll swim back to shore naked."

"Deal!" I said before I could even think.

"Okay, on my count. 3 . . . 2 . . . 1 . . . go!" Dakin was off, and I could have sworn that he had superpowered webbed feet or something. I felt like a toddler splashing around in a baby pool, but that didn't stop me, though. I splashed and kicked as hard and fast as I could.

Unfortunately, I was at least three lengths behind Dakin. He rested his arms on the pier and waited for me.

Breathless, I reached for the wood to give my legs a rest.

"How?" was all I could manage, still huffing and puffing.

"I'm bigger, stronger, and just better at everything."

I stuck out my tongue at him and he just laughed.

"Man, winning makes a man hungry."

I splashed him as he started swimming back to the shore. Groaning and still puffing from the exertion I put myself through, I followed him back to our picnic.

When I eventually came back on land, Dakin was already drying off. He tossed a towel my way. I muttered a thanks and started drying my face. Patting the rest of my body dry, I wrapped the towel around me and sat down on the blanket, ready to devour the meal Ryker and I had prepared.

As we ate, I saw a brother and sister running amok around the edge of the water. They each held a water gun, try to dodge the other's blast whenever a spray let loose. Laughing and playing, they ran up and down the shore, and I couldn't help but smile at them.

"Remember when we used to be like that?" Dakin asked, already digging into the second sandwich.

"Young and naïve? Without a care in the world?"

"Yeah. Those sure were the days."

"I would have agreed with you on that, but lately it feels more like a dream than a memory." I grabbed a can of soda, opened it, and took a big gulp.

"I hear ya. Before the magic and mayhem, everything seemed simpler."

"Tell me about it." I rolled my eyes as I finished my sandwich. Dakin had demolished his second sandwich. How could he eat so much and stay so thin? "Can I ask you a question?" I asked as I brushed crumbs off the blanket.

"Shoot."

"When did you learn about this world?"

Dakin thought about it for a moment, his brow furrowed. "I guess I've always known. My parents never tried to hide it from me. I do remember, though, when I was small, probably just before we met, my parents told me we weren't like normal people. That we had an affinity for animals. Guess being a familiar is why we are so good with the rescues."

"Makes sense. You can be a dog just like the rest of them," I mocked playfully.

Dakin responded with a growl and a bark that sent us both into a fit of laughter and me trying to teach him tricks with a bag of opened potato chips.

After I refused to give him a chip, he tackled me to the sand and started licking my face, pretending all too well to be the dog I suggested he was. I pushed him off me in a fit of hysterics and we both lay on our backs. When the fun died down and I wiped my face with my towel, I had another thought.

"Do you think things will change much in the future? Do you think the power will corrupt me?"

"That would never happen. I won't let it. I'm your familiar, and as long as I'm around, I won't ever let you go dark." He squeezed my hand, and we stared at the cloudless sky in silence, the sun warming our cool bodies from the swim.

We lay there for a long while until Dakin stood and tugged me to my feet. "Why don't we go get that boat ride I won?"

"Oh, you mean the one you cheated on?"

"Hey, if being better at everything is called cheating, then yes."

We walked toward the docked rowing boats and took one out onto the water. It felt unstable until Dakin and I were settled in, and he was rowing to the center of the lake.

"Row, row, row your boat, gently down the stream . . ." Dakin started singing very off-key as he plunged the oars into the water and maneuvered us around.

"You do know that that song is actually a song about death, right? About rowing toward the afterlife in Greek mythology?"

Dakin just shrugged and put the oars away as we drifted gently around the lake.

"You know, you shouldn't be so hard on Mae. Not everything is as you deem it, and maybe it was harder on her than you think."

"Why? Why did you have to bring that up now? We were having such a good time." I couldn't even storm off in annoyance.

Nice move, Dakin.

"I know, but after this day is over, you'll still need to deal with it."

"I'll deal with it as I see fit."

"How? By getting defensive? Listen to yourself. This is not you." Dakin tried calming the storm he'd stirred inside of me.

"What do you know about any of this? How would you know what Mae has been feeling or dealing with?" I crossed my arms, hugging myself. I didn't want to hear his reply.

"I know because I was doing the same thing. To be honest, I was asked to keep an eye on you before Mae. You know, since I'm your familiar and all."

"What? Are you telling me you've been Ryker's spy as well? For how long?" Anger burned within like a hot iron, ready to be driven into bare flesh.

"Amy . . . This is not—"

"How long!" I shouted.

The boat started rocking from side to side.

"Amy—"

"Tell me!"

The boat swayed aggressively from side to side.

"Amy, please! You need to calm down before you throw us both overboard."

I shook my head. I wasn't the cause of the motion.

"I can't . . . . It's not me." I gripped the sides of the boat as it swayed even more. Before we could say or do anything else, the boat capsized.

CHAPTER 15

I hit the water. The icy chill made me gasp, and I swallowed a mouthful of lake water. It disoriented me from knowing which way was up and which way was down. I started kicking and swaying my arms to get some traction in the water. Thankfully, I could see the sun shining above me. I swam toward the light and broke through the water . . . right underneath the capsized boat.

"Amy! Amy, where are you?" Dakin's faint voice called from the other side of the boat.

"Dakin! I'm okay. I'm under the boat."

"Are you okay?" His voice became clearer as he neared.

"I'm fine. What happened?"

"I have no idea." None of it made sense. I was about to dive underwater to get out from under the boat, when a strange sensation occurred around me.

It started as a small whirlpool underwater, like one of those air pockets jellyfish get caught in. A neon blue light surrounded the air pocket, but nothing about this felt like a natural occurrence.

"Dakin?"

"I'm here."

"Something's wrong. Something's happening. I don't know what to do." I tried to kick at the whirling water around my feet, but it only broke apart and reformed, like one of those plasma creatures in horror movies.

"Hang on, I'm coming."

Before I could reply, the water amoeba tied itself around my lower legs and started pulling me under.

I tried to fight, to hang on to the seats on the overturned boat, but the current was too strong. I screeched as it pulled me under and backwards toward the shore.

Thinking of the water magic Ryker had taught me, I tried using spells to help, but the fear of what was happening rendered my magic useless. Swimming didn't help, either. The more I fought, the stronger the pull came.

I saw Dakin swimming toward me underwater. His eyes bulged as he saw the whirling current surrounding me. With a speed I didn't know he had, he reached me within seconds and grabbed my wrists.

As he pulled, I tried kicking at the air pockets again, but nothing seemed to help. The current eased a bit, but the strange water moved from my body and knocked Dakin back so far that he couldn't follow me.

As the whirlpool tightened its grip on me again, I saw the shimmer of magic surrounding it. My last thought before it tugged me toward shore again was: *Fuck*.

The pull increased, and suddenly I was thrown on to the shore. I coughed up water, gasping for air. The sand beneath my hands turned to mushy water dripping from my body. I looked at the lake and saw a tiny glimmer of a human shape in the distance, swimming avidly toward me. Dakin.

I pushed to my feet, ignoring my quivering muscles. As I made my way to the water to get back to Dakin, a powerful hand clamped down on my shoulder, accompanied by a deep and rusty voice.

"You're coming with me."

As if by nature, Ryker's training took over. I stepped to the side and turned around, lifting my arm and wrapping it around the man's arm, whose hand was still clamped on my shoulder. I locked my wrist at the man's elbow, placing my other hand on the man's shoulder, then I kicked his knee, making him unstable in his stance. I pushed him down, pulling the arm I had in a lock to the sky, forcing him to the ground.

When he hit the ground, I placed my knee on his shoulder, pushing him further into the ground, replacing the hand that was there, and used all my strength to dislocate his shoulder. The man screamed in pain as the shoulder popped beneath my knee. I stood up and let the man roll over onto his back, clutching his arm. He wanted to sit up and curse me, but before he could say anything, my fist connected with his face, knocking him out cold.

The adrenaline spike in my system didn't make me feel the pain, but I knew it would come soon. I stood over the unconscious man for a few seconds, trying to see if he looked familiar, when another man grabbed me from behind.

Instincts said to use my head, so I did, but instead of making contact with a nose, I only hit the attacker's chest.

Shit!

When the man lifted me, I knew he was taller than the one I'd knocked out. His grip tightened around me as I squirmed, trying to slip away, and I struggled to breathe. He moved with me in his grasp, as if I weighed nothing. This would not be easy.

I took a deep breath, trying to calm my busy mind to help me focus. I hooked my one foot behind the attacker's knee and held it there. The guy stopped moving and tried to shake me loose, but I stayed in place.

Knowing that this guy was way too tall and I wouldn't be able to kick at his groin like Ryker had showed me, I reverted to the knee instead. I brought my knee up to my chest and, with as much force as I could muster, kicked at the man's knee. As a pop sounded around us, the attacker dropped me.

Thank goodness for all the balance training I had done, as I immediately turned around. Using the momentum of the spin, I kicked his groin, making him bend over. I pulled the foot back in an almost-lunge and drove my knee into his face repeatedly while grabbing his head, keeping it in place.

As my knee made contact with his nose, I heard the cracking sound and saw the blood running over my body to the ground. The man screamed in agony from the pain.

Without hesitation, I brought him in closer, lifted my arm as high as I could, and drove my elbow to the back of his head. His body went limp, and I knew he was either asleep or dead, but all I could think about was getting away.

My breathing came out rapidly as I scanned the surrounding area for more attackers. There were none.

I heard a splashing sound and heard my name being called from the water. Turning around, I saw Dakin struggling to run to me through the shallow waves.

I ran toward Dakin, meeting him as the water decreased to his calves. I threw my arms around him and hugged him to me. He instinctively wrapped his arms around me and just held me.

"Are you okay?" Dakin broke the hug and moved his hands to my face, inspecting me for any injuries.

I nodded, wondering if I had any pain.

Dakin pulled me in for another hug and whispered, "I think you're more than okay." He chuckled.

I pulled away from him and looked to where he gestured.

On the ground lay the unconscious bodies of my two assailants. Looking at them now, it surprised me at how big they actually were. I couldn't help but laugh at the thought that I, a tiny girl, had taken on those two and won.

"Looks like Ryker's training actually paid off."

"Looks that way. Remind me to never get on your bad side."

"Shit. I have to phone Ryker."

I walked to our picnic area and started drying off and getting dressed. There was no way that I'd be staying at the lake any longer. Almost as if reading my mind, Dakin started getting dressed and packing up our things. I grabbed my phone and dialed Ryker's number.

As I waited for him to pick up, I looked around the area and saw that it was deserted. Where had everyone gone? The phone rang a few times and then went to voicemail. I dialed his number again. A few rings later, it went to voicemail again. An uneasy feeling settled over me as I dialed a third time. Still, after a few rings the automated voice came, saying that the person I was trying to contact was unavailable. I ended the call and looked at Dakin. Anxiety and fear settled into my solar plexus.

"Ryker's not answering. Something's wrong."

CHAPTER 16

*H*astily, we packed up our things from the shore and headed through the trees toward the parking area. Dakin's truck was parked in the second row of the lot, all alone. Not a vehicle was in sight. It was weird. When we had headed out in the boat, there had been so many people around, but now it was as if everyone just disappeared.

Dakin put all the bags in the back of the truck as I climbed in. I was struggling with the seatbelt because my hands were shaking too much. Dakin took one look at me as he got settled, then took my hands in his.

"I know what you're feeling, but this won't help you." He gave my hands a small kiss, trying to calm my nerves. As he let go, he clipped my seatbelt for me. He started the truck and pulled out of the parking lot as I fumbled with my phone, trying Ryker again.

"Maybe he forgot his phone at home?" I said out loud, mostly to myself, trying to persuade myself that Ryker could be forgetful and that everything would be fine. Taking a deep, shaky breath, I dialed another number.

"I wondered when I would hear from you again," Mae's sing-song voice came through the phone. Without saying hi or saying something along the lines of an apology or snarky comment, my mind went to one thing only.

"Is Ryker there?"

"Sorry?"

"Is Ryker there?" I asked again, panic settling in with every breath. "I tried phoning him a few times but he's not picking up."

"No, he's not here. Amy, what's wrong?" she asked, noticing the fear in my voice.

I told her about the two Tainted goons who had attacked me, and that they'd used magic to pull me underwater and towards the shore.

"Are you okay, babes? How did you get rid of them?"

"Ryker's training. But that's beside the point. Mae, where is Ryker? It's not like him to not be available when I call. Especially since he told me to call."

"Okay, calm down, hun. Where are you now?"

"Dakin and I are on our way home. Mae, I have a bad feeling about all of this." I shared a look with Dakin, and he increased the speed. It was like he could feel it, too.

"I'm locking up the shop now. I'll meet you at home. Everything will be fine."

"I hope so." Without a goodbye, I disconnected the call.

The lake wasn't far from home, but the drive seemed to take an eternity. My mind was reeling with the possibilities of what had happened. Was Ryker okay? Was he in danger? Did he need my help? Had something bad happened to him? Just the thought of it all made my throat tighten, and I had to fight to keep the tears at bay. I didn't want to think about it, but I couldn't stop myself from thinking about it.

I knew Dakin wanted to say something, but he seemed to know that nothing he'd say would help the situation. So, he just stared ahead, gripping the steering wheel, driving as fast as he dared to get me to Ryker.

The main road came into view. Cars lined the sides, people wandered around, dwindling in and out of the shops, talking and enjoying their day. None of them were aware of the dangers lurking around the corners of their mundane lives.

Dakin took a turn toward my street, trying to avoid pedestrians walking across the road. Families enjoyed the day in the park, but whenever I looked at the park, the day of my attack flashed through my mind. How things had changed since then.

We turned onto my street, and my agitation grew as I watched the house slowly come into view. Dakin started slacking off when we neared, and before he had come to a complete stop, I opened the door and jumped out, hearing Dakin calling to me.

"Amy, wait!"

I didn't look back. My only thought was to get to Ryker. To ensure he was fine, that nothing was wrong. Just thinking about it made my stomach churn. I knew it was a false hope that I was trying to convince myself of.

I rushed across the lawn, skipping the two steps to the porch, then I skidded to a halt. The front door stood ajar. The wood below the handle was scuffed, and splintered wood stuck out of the door at the side. I wanted to go inside, but my body held back. I was afraid of what I would find.

Dakin rushed over to me, the truck's keys dangling in his hand as he came to a rest right behind me. I looked at him, then at the door. Without another word, Dakin stepped in front of me and led the way into the house.

I called out Ryker's name, but all that answered was silence. The only sound in the house was me and Dakin walking through the house.

My voice caught in my throat as we stepped into the living room.

Half of the furniture was uprooted and strewn across the room. Broken glassware littered the floor, a clear sign of a struggle. I called Ryker's name again, but there was still no answer.

"I'll check the rooms," Dakin said, heading toward the bedrooms. I walked through the living room, stepping over pillows and broken portraits.

In the dining room, the table was no longer in the center of the room but rather pushed against the wall. Half the chairs were turned upside down and scattered throughout the room. One chair was broken into pieces and its leg had been impaled into a painting on the wall.

What the hell happened here?

"Ryker!" I called again.

Glass crunched under my shoes as I walked, and I glanced down. I froze. There were red smears on the floor.

Blood.

Panic filled me. Whatever happened here hadn't ended well for someone. I entered the kitchen, and a muted scream left me. Ryker lay on the kitchen floor, blood pooling underneath him.

I ran toward him, skidding on my hands and knees, his blood sticky on my skin. I called his name and touched his face, trying to wake him, but nothing seemed to work. I yelled for Dakin as I lifted Ryker's head onto my lap.

I stroked his face while I spoke to him, but when my hand traveled to his hair and came back bloody, I yelled at Dakin to call 911. I put my fingers to his neck, then his wrist, checking for a pulse. It was faint, but it was still there.

Dakin rushed into the kitchen. With a quick glance at the mess, he pulled out his phone and called an ambulance. I cradled Ryker's head on my lap, rocking him back and forth like he used to rock me when I had been injured as a child.

"Stay with me, Ryker, please. Help is on the way, just stay with me," I murmured, knowing that he if he could hear me, he would stay with me.

A feminine voice called through house, and I looked up as Mae stormed into the kitchen. . She gasped at the sight of me sitting in a pool of blood, holding Ryker's head in my lap. I sobbed, and the tears I'd managed to hold at bay tracked down my cheeks. Mae was at my side in an instant, handing me a dishtowel and guiding my hand to the wound on Ryker's head. I couldn't put my feelings into words. I just stared at Mae, and she nodded, knowing exactly what it was that I wanted to say.

"I'm here. Everything will be okay. Just stay with me, please. I don't know what I would do if you left me, too." Tears streamed down my face in full force, blurring my sight of Ryker as I rocked him back and forth, whispering the words on repeat.

Sirens echoed through the air. Help was coming.

But the pit in my stomach told me help was just an illusion.

CHAPTER 17

Dakin showed the paramedics into the house and to me and Ryker.

"What happened here?" one paramedic asked Dakin.

"I don't know. We found him like this."

I zoned out as they asked Dakin more questions. They set a gurney down, and one of the paramedics sat down on Ryker's other side.

"Miss, I'm going to need you to move, please. We'll take care of him."

I looked at the woman. She had dark skin and the softest brown eyes anyone would be able to drown in. Her curly, black hair was pulled tight into a ponytail and bounced as she spoke. She touched my arm gently.

"Amy, the paramedics need to work." Mae came to my side and started pulling me to stand. I shrugged her off. I didn't want to leave Ryker's side.

"Amy, please," she pleaded with me, still trying to pull me away. "Ryker needs them to help. They can't help him if you're in the way."

I looked at Mae, then back down at Ryker, his head resting on the ground. I looked at the female paramedic, who nodded at me as she held a small flashlight in her hands, shining it into Ryker's eyes.

Reluctantly, I stood up and moved away from Ryker's unconscious body. The other paramedic took my place and started taking Ryker's blood pressure. The two medics spoke to one another as they started working on my uncle.

Standing to the side of the kitchen, my eyes never left the scene in front of me. Even if I wanted to look away, I couldn't.

This wasn't right. This should have never happened. If I hadn't gone to the lake, I could've been here to save him, to protect him. Mae wrapped her arm around my shoulders. The pressure of the gesture made me want to break down and cry, but all I did was let the tears fall. I couldn't help it and didn't have the energy to wipe them away.

Mae held me tight in a sideways hug, rubbing my shoulders every now and then when a sob threatened to escape me. Dakin came to stand on my other side and handed me tissues. I looked at him, and he just nodded with clear tenderness in his eyes. I mouthed a "thank you" as I took it and dabbed at the tears streaming freely down my face like an overflowing river.

Just as I thought the medics were almost done with Ryker, he started convulsing. The paramedics spoke to each other, throwing around jargon I didn't understand, and worked even faster. Instinct took over, and I wanted to run over, shove the paramedics away and hold Ryker.

As if he knew what I was thinking, Dakin grabbed me around my waist and held me back against him as I fought to get free. Mae stood in front of me and put her hands on my shoulders.

"Amy, listen to me. You need to calm yourself. Interfering with the paramedics won't help Ryker." Over her shoulder, I saw the medics inject Ryker with a medicine that helped with the seizure. I let some of the tension in my body ease as I nodded and sank back against Dakin, not taking my eyes off the scene in front of me.

"I think we should wait outside until they're done here." Mae spoke more to Dakin than to me, and then he was pulling me out of the room. When I glanced back at Ryker, I could have sworn a shimmer surrounded him, but when I checked again, it was gone.

It must have been a reflection on one of the apparatuses, but somehow my mind refused to believe it. Something about all this just seemed wrong.

As we walked through the house to get outside, all I noticed was destruction. From this side of the house, it looked much worse. Then again, when I came in, my primary purpose had been to find Ryker. Now that I was no longer thinking about it, I could see the chaos.

My mind was going all *Fast Five* on me now, wondering how it was even possible. Ryker was gifted in hand-to-hand combat and a very powerful magic user.

Outside, the first thing I noticed was the ambulance standing on the street, lights flickering through the neighborhood. People stood in the street, just staring, probably talking about what they thought was happening here. Just thinking about everyone gossiping increased my anger level, and I wanted to scream at them all to go off and mind their own business.

We stood outside for a while, my emotions ranging from stress and worry about Ryker and anger toward the damn, nosy neighbors. The medics came out of the house, one pulling the gurney while the other one pushed it. Ryker lay on top of it, the IV resting on the blanket, and an oxygen mask covering most of his face.

Fresh tears fell from my eyes as I watched them load Ryker into the ambulance.

"Amy, why don't you ride in the ambulance? Dakin and I will meet you at the hospital." Mae pushed me in the direction of the van, where the female paramedic waited for me. I gripped the steel handlebars and pulled myself up.

The scent of disinfectant and soap burned my stomach. The aroma churned my stomach, and I was dangerously close to vomiting.

"You get used to the smell," the woman said, smiling at me. She worked over Ryker, adjusting machines and locking the bed into place. Once she was satisfied that she had done everything, she knocked on the steel frame, and the ambulance started.

She gestured for me to sit on the small bench next to the gurney as she took her own seat near front, close to Ryker's head. The sirens of the ambulance sounded from on top of the van, but it wasn't as loud from the inside as I would have expected.

I moved in closer as tears filled my eyes. If it wasn't for the machines beeping over the silence and the fact that Ryker's chest was moving, I would have thought he was dead. Just the thought of it sent the tears over the edge.

gripped Ryker's hand between mine, scared that if I let go of him, it would be the last time. I couldn't even think about it without the gut-wrenching feeling of grief and loss wallowing inside me.

"I'm so sorry. I don't know if you can hear me, I hope you can," I began as I held on to his hand. There was no reaction whatsoever. I glanced at the paramedic, but she was preoccupied with other things. Maybe she just wanted to give me some privacy and was pretending to do things. I looked back to Ryker. His face showed the signs of a fight.

Bruises were forming around his eye, and the discoloration continued down his cheek. The lacerations on his nose and lips looked painful, and my heart clenched in my chest. It hurt to see him like this.

"It's all my fault. If you could, I know you'd tell me that it's not my fault. That nothing I could have done could have prevented this from happening. That if I had been there, things might have turned out worse, but to me, right now . . . this is the worst.

"I don't care what you say, or would've said, but I should have been there. I shouldn't have gone to the lake with Dakin. If I had been home, then I could have helped you fight. I could have protected you like you have done for me my entire life. Maybe they wouldn't have been there at all if we were together. We are always stronger together." I glanced up at the paramedic, then lowered my voice.

"Maybe if I wasn't the last Pure, then this wouldn't have happened. The Tainted wouldn't have been searching for me. All this trouble would never have come to pass. Hell, if I wasn't a Pure at all, our lives would have been completely different. I'm so sorry for causing you all this pain. It's all my fault." Tears streamed down my face like a raging rapid seeking escape, and I let them. I needed to get all of this out of my mind and off my chest.

All the emotions consumed me at once. I couldn't distinguish the one from the other. Was it anxiety, stress, worry? Was I distressed about Ryker or about what had happened at the lake? Maybe it was a combination of both, or it could have been something else entirely.

Something inside me called out, saying that something else was coming. Something horrible and terrifying, and no matter what we did, no one would be prepared for it. Just the thought of what might be coming sent my anxiety through the ambulance roof.

I squeezed Ryker's hand tighter with every thought that whirled through my mind. Even though he couldn't say anything, just having him close was comforting.

The ambulance slowed down, then stopped. I heard noises from the outside and jumped when the doors opened to the emergency room. Doctors stood outside, prepared to take Ryker from the ambulance. So many people were bustling about, talking about things that made little sense to me. The two medics lowered the gurney out of the ambulance and told them their preliminary diagnoses.

They rolled Ryker through the open doors into an examination room for observation. There were so many people working around Ryker that I couldn't even distinguish between the doctors and the nurses.

They were shouting over each other, but they all seemed to understand what was being said. I didn't envy the nurses. The doctors yelled for IV bags of O-neg. They shone lights in Ryker's eyes and gave feedback about scans while one of them called out his blood pressure.

I couldn't even keep track. I didn't know what they were talking about, so I didn't know what the hell was happening.

"What's happening?" I asked to anyone who was willing on helping me, but I got no response. "Can anyone tell me if Ryker is okay?" I asked again, but the doctors ignored me.

I stepped closer, reiterating my question. A doctor turned and stared at me in astonishment.

"Get her out of here, now!" he barked at a nurse.

The nurse hurried over to me and pulled away, closing the curtain on the scene.

"Come on, sweetie, you can wait in the waiting area and let the good doctors do their job." She pulled me away but before we could get anywhere out of sight, the monitors beeped and the doctors yelled, "Code blue." The nurse that was with me let go of my arm and immediately went to go help.

I was no medical professional, but I had seen enough *Grey's Anatomy* to know that 'code blue' meant there was no pulse. Worried out of my mind, I turned back toward the curtain. The one doctor was half on top of Ryker, giving him CPR.

"We need an OR, stat!" he yelled as he kept up the compressions on Ryker's chest, not even stopping for a second.

"What's happening? What's going on?"

"Get her out of here!" the doctor yelled. They pushed me out of the way as they unlocked the wheels of the bed and pushed it toward the elevator. Probably heading up to the operating room. I followed behind the rush.

Was I invisible? Why was everyone just ignoring me? What the hell? I started hyperventilating again. My chest constricted and I couldn't breathe. No matter how hard I tried to inhale, no oxygen seemed to be getting into my lungs.

I watched the group of doctors hurry into the elevator and saw it close behind them. It all happened like a movie. The world started spinning; the people were walking past me, hardly giving me a simple glance.

A nurse, the same one as before, came toward me. She took hold of my elbow, and I could hear her asking something, but the sound was muffled like the teacher from the peanuts cartoons.

"I-can't-breathe," I huffed as the room spun and everything went dark.

"I need some help over here!" the nurse called.

Colors flashed before me. Golds and blues tinted the edges of my vision. Water trickled down somewhere. The sound of birds singing felt like they were flying right in front of me.

I didn't know where I was, but I felt a tremendous sense of peace. Everything was simplistic, harmonious, gentle. There was no worry or stress. No wanting or needing. It was like this was where I belonged.

"Not yet, child." Colors danced in front of my eyes as a woman's voice sounded in my head. It was so loud and clear that I could have sworn she was standing right by my ear.

"What do you mean not yet?" I asked, trying to find the source, but I only saw darkness.

"It is not yet time for you to stay here." The colors danced with her voice. It almost seemed like it was her and she was it. "Correct."

"Who are you? How do you know my thoughts?"

"I am the mother of all my children. I am the beat underneath your feet. The vibration in every thought, the energy of nature. I am Gaia." With that, she appeared in a flash that I was awestruck.

The mother goddess stood in front of me, clothed in pure white, with a golden aura surrounding her. Her brown, curled hair cascaded down her olive skin as she stood in front of a magnificent golden temple.

As quickly as she appeared, she disappeared.

"The time for you to wake up is now," she whispered.

I tried to follow her voice, but I was running into darkness, going nowhere. As the colors of her energy left me, I heard voices that did not belong to Gaia, nor did the sounds.

"No, please, wait! I have so much to ask you," I cried into the nothingness, hoping I could find one more second of her presence, but only emptiness greeted me.

The voices became louder, accompanied by soft beeping sounds. I shook my head, trying to get rid of the unfamiliar noise that did not belong.

"I think she's waking up," a female voice said, and I wanted to scream at her for being so close to me, for waking me up. I wanted to stay here.

"Amy? Can you hear me?" a male voice asked, and I felt a pressure on my hand.

What was this? What was happening to me? I closed my eyes, trying to force them away from me.

When I opened my eyes again, a bright light from the ceiling greeted me . . . from my bed in the hospital.

CHAPTER 19

"She's awake! Get the nurse," a male voice said next to me with a hint of urgency. It sounded familiar, but I couldn't place it. I didn't want to. I wanted to be back there with Gaia. It was so beautiful and serene. Peaceful.

My eyes focused as I looked around. I was on a bed with the curtains drawn around it. I saw Mae leave behind the one curtain. Turning my head, I saw Dakin sitting on my right. I wanted to talk, but my voice sounded muffled. As I lifted my hand to feel on my face, Dakin grabbed my hand and held it in his.

"No, leave it on."

With my left hand, I felt about my face. A silicone mask covered my mouth. I pulled it down to speak properly.

"What happened?"

"You had a panic attack and fainted from hyperventilation."

I groaned, balling the mask in my fist. "I wish I would stop doing that. I'm not a damsel in distress."

"Well, you do kind of have a flair for the dramatics." Dakin shrugged.

I untucked my hand from his and gave him an Andre Agassi backhand.

He rubbed at his arm in fake pain and leaned in closer to me. "I think you've spent too much time with Mae. You picked up on all her melodramatics." I giggled at the way he said it, checking over his shoulder for the devil to arrive. "Don't tell her I said anything."

"Don't tell who what?" Mae entered the curtained off room followed by a nurse.

"Nothing," Dakin replied sheepishly, and Mae looked at him with a raised eyebrow, knowing full well that he was talking about her.

"How are you feeling, sweetie?" The nurse came to my bedside and took my stats, not making eye contact.

"I'm fine now, thank you. How is Ryker doing?"

"That's good to hear. Your uncle has been taken to the OR, but if you'd like, you and your friends"—she enunciated the word 'friends', giving me the impression that she wasn't that fond of them—"can head to the cafeteria for a bite to eat and then wait in the waiting room until a doctor has updated you." It sounded more like a demand than a suggestion. I just nodded, and the nurse was out the cubicle.

"Remind me to never get on her bad side," Mae mumbled. She handed me a small bag from underneath the bed. "Here, thought you could use a change of clothes. The ones you have . . . well, let's just say you can't go out in public with them." I looked down at my clothes and saw that they were stained with dried blood.

"Thank you," I whispered, glad that someone had thought about a change of clothes for me. I would have never even thought to look at my appearance. I struggled upright, and Dakin and Mae were at my sides immediately, trying to help me.

"I'm fine, really. It was a simple panic attack, not a heart attack. Can I have some privacy, please?" I asked, sitting up and clutching the bag Mae had brought. I could see her wanting to protest, but Dakin grabbed her by the elbow and pulled her along. Some choice words left her mouth at that action.

"We'll meet you in the cafeteria," Dakin said before he pulled the curtain closed behind him. I sat back against my pillow and blew out a breath. It felt like I had been holding that breath since what had happened at the lake.

I lay back against the bed, letting my mind process everything that had happened in the last few days. Mae's truth that felt like a betrayal, my almost-nuclear magical explosion, the truth at the lake about Dakin's secrets, the lake attack itself, finding Ryker. It was all too overwhelming.

My breath quivered as I let tears fall freely down my cheeks. All my emotions needed an escape, and this was the safest way. I let everything go—the hurt, betrayal, worry, stress, the everything.

Grabbing hold of the blanket, I pulled it to my face, hoping that it would help muffle my sobs. My shoulders shook as I cried everything out. When I was all cried out, I knew I couldn't stay there and wallow in my sorrow. I needed to do something.

I grabbed the bag Mae had packed for me and made my way down the hall to the bathroom. Once inside, I made sure that the door was locked and nearly dropped the bag to the floor when I saw my reflection in the mirror.

I was covered in blood—a ghostly version of myself. My eyes were puffy from crying, circled with red from rubbing the tears with my bloodstained hands.

I opened the tap and did my best to scrub the stains from my hands. The water ran down the drain in a pink liquid until it was clear, but I kept rubbing, hoping that the more I scrubbed, the memories that I knew would haunt me would rub off and disappear into the unknown abyss of the sewer.

Next, I tried to tackle my face. I shed myself of my bloody clothes and tossed them into the bin. There was no way in hell I would be able to salvage them. I grabbed paper towels from the dispensary, soaked them with water and soap, and started cleaning up the mess on my face, my arms, the hollow of my neck and my legs.

The more I cleaned, the more I wanted to clean. I rubbed my entire body until it burned from the friction, reveling in the pain that it brought me as my anger at the sight of it made me want to injure the people responsible for what happened to Ryker.

When I was sure that everything was semi-cleaned, and that if I continued to scrub, I would have no skin left, I tossed the bloody towels in the garbage bin and got dressed in the clothes that Mae had brought me.

I noticed in the bag that she had also brought me a hairbrush and some hair ties. Only a girl would think of things like that. I grabbed the brush and yanked it through my hair, trying to tame it into something half presentable, then tied it back in a ponytail. Placing the brush back into the bag, I noticed Mae had packed my skincare products—face wash, moisturizer, and an ointment that helped with puffy eyes. She'd really thought of everything.

It took me about thirty minutes to use the things that Mae packed, but when I was done and ready to leave the bathroom, I looked more like myself than I had an hour ago, even if I didn't feel like it.

Zipping up the bag, I took one last look at my reflection and left the bathroom and all the bloodstained memories with it.

The hospital buzzed with activity as doctors and nurses slipped past me, not even giving me a sideways glance as they raced with a tablet in hand to the next emergency. I followed the boards on the wall to the cafeteria.

Once I got there, I saw Mae and Dakin already seated at a table, deep in discussion.

"I swear to you, Newt's coffee is by far the best," Mae argued, gesturing to the cup in front of her.

"And I'm telling you it tastes exactly the same as this," Dakin countered, grinning at me as I stepped closer.

"What do you think, Aims?" Mae asked as I sat down, placing the sort-of-empty bag at my feet.

"Think about what?"

"That Newt's coffee is way better than this stuff."

"Does it have caffeine in?" I asked, not really in the mood for small talk, but I'd rather amuse them than deal with the hell my life had become. They both looked at me and nodded. "Well, if it has caffeine in, then I say, who the hell cares? You can't really taste the difference."

"You guys know nothing of what good coffee tastes like." Mae huffs, folding her arms across her chest. She always did that when she knew she was fighting a losing battle.

"Oh, come now, be honest. It's not the coffee you like, but the owner," Dakin mocked.

Mae wanted to protest but said nothing.

"Wait. Do you have a crush on Newt?" I asked, half surprised, half joking.

"No! Don't be absurd," Mae protested, but the blush in her cheeks gave away the secret.

"Oh, my! Mae! What the—You never told me this."

"There's nothing to tell!"

"Then why are you blushing?"

"I—" Mae turned beetroot as she tried to defend her status, but her words failed her.

"I can't believe you have a crush on the barista owner." I laughed out loud, and for a while, I forget we were at the hospital, and why.

"That's why you keep getting those 'loyalty' discounts." Dakin air-quoted as he kept mocking Mae. He was having way too much fun with it.

A waitress stopped by and handed me a cup of coffee. Dakin and Mae must have told her to hand me a cup when I arrived. After adding some sugar and milk, I took a sip and laughed through mouthful as Dakin kept pulling Mae's leg about the crush.

In a way, I could see Mae's fascination with the barista owner. Newt was sweet and caring, loyal to a fault, and saw opportunities where normal people saw obstacles. He wasn't bad looking—if you liked the whole nerdy hacker look. Wasn't my type at all, but what kind of friend would I be if I shunned a choice that my best friend made?

As I sipped on my coffee and watched the scene between Mae and

Dakin unfold, I noticed two police officers walking toward us. Keeping my eye on them, I saw them walking to our table and a nervous feeling settled inside my stomach as they reached us.

"Which one of you is Amunet Wicc?"

CHAPTER 20

*H*esitating, I lifted my hand and indicated to the police officers that they were looking for me.

"We'd like to ask you some questions," the taller of the two said as he removed his hat and cradled it underneath his arm while taking out a small notepad to write on.

I nodded and looked at Dakin and Mae.

"We'll be waiting outside for you." Mae mentioned to Dakin to leave, and both my friends stood, leaving me with the cops. The nervous sensations returned as the cops took over the seats that my friends had vacated.

"Miss Wicc," the one officer began, clicking his pen so that he could write. "Would you mind telling us where you were today?"

"Um, I was with my friend at the lake from around nine this morning."

"When was the last time you spoke with your uncle?"

"This morning. He dropped me off at the lake and told me to call when he should come and pick me up, but he never answered his phone."

"Is that unusual?" the one police officer asked.

I looked at his partner, who scribbled in the notebook.

"Sort of. My uncle is a bit of a paranoid individual when it comes to me."

"How so?"

"He's always been protective. So, when I called, and he didn't answer after the third attempt, I knew something was wrong."

"I see," the officer said, tapping the pen to his lips. They were trying to play good cop/bad cop, but I had nothing to hide.

"Do you know of anyone that would want to hurt your uncle?"

I thought about his question, maybe longer than I would have liked, but I couldn't tell the police about the Tainted or about the mystical world that they were probably oblivious to.

"My uncle is a bookstore owner and an antiques specialist. Who would ever want to harm an academic? Makes no sense to me." I knew I was laying it on a bit thick, but it made sense. Or so I hoped.

"That's a nasty cut you've got there." The one police officer motioned to my head.

Without even thinking, my hand traveled to my forehead, and I winced as my fingers grazed across the cut that started at my hairline and ended in the middle of my forehead. Gauze covered the wound, and I suspected that the nurses must have cleaned it after I fainted. The police officer's gaze held mine, and I immediately removed my hand from my head and curled it around the cold coffee mug.

"It must have happened at the lake," I answered the unasked question. When the raised eyebrow indicated the officer needed more information, I obliged. "My friend and I went out on the water with a rowboat. The water got rough, probably from all the activity on the lake, and the boat tipped over. I must have hit my head when that happened."

"And you didn't notice it right away?"

What was with the suspicions?

"When I came up for air, I was underneath the capsized boat. The water was freezing, so no, I did not feel it." I glared at the bad cop.

"Excuse me? Miss Wicc?" I looked up at the fresh voice. A doctor stood at the table, dressed in blue scrubs and a white coat.

"Yes?" I answered, sounding unsure. The nerves started eating at me in fear of bad news.

"My name is Doctor Spencer. Your uncle is out of surgery and in recovery right now. He had some swelling on the brain, but we elevated the pressure." The doctor looked at the two police officers, then back at me.

"Can I see him?" I asked, ignoring the cops.

The doctor stared at the cops again, probably wanting to know if it would be okay.

"I think we have enough information now. We'll call you if we have any more questions." The good cop stood and nodded in my direction while the bad cop still glared at me. I had a strange feeling about that man, and not that he thought I was guilty. His energy just seemed off.

"Please follow me." The doctor gestured as he turned around.

I stood, leaving the half-empty cup on the table, and followed the dark-haired man down the hallway.

"Your uncle isn't awake yet, but that is to be expected with a head injury. Luckily, there weren't any major damages, so when the swelling goes down and we've patched him up again, he'll be able to go home," Doctor Spencer said as he led me to a room.

I wanted to thank him, but the good doctor just patted my shoulder sympathetically and strode off toward the nurses' station.

The hallways were a light color, with linoleum floors stretching throughout the space. Doctors and nurses hustled around. Some were talking to family members, while others were either filling out paperwork or talking to other medical professionals. Standing like a lost soul in the doorway, I felt like a ghost, watching everything around me, not being noticed. Taking a deep breath, I turned toward Ryker's room and headed inside.

The room seemed as dark as my emotions, even with the bright fluorescents shining overhead. Two windows on the opposite side of the door stared out into the darkness of the evening sky as a small empty table awaited gifts or flowers for the patient. Against the one wall, a door was closed, probably hiding a small en-suite bathroom behind. Medical equipment took over the rest of the room.

My gaze drifted to the bed Ryker was on and a lump formed in my throat. The hospital bed stood high, and thin blankets had been draped over Ryker, barely covering his body enough for any kind of heat. Machines stood on both sides, beeping with his pulse into the eerie silence of the room. Tubes and wires entangled their way from the machines toward Ryker, making him look trapped inside the nest of cabling that was saving his life.

I stepped closer to the only chair available for me to sit on and planted myself on it. All the emotions from that day rushed through me, and I felt so overwhelmed that I couldn't contain myself. Despair and remorse clutched at my heart as I picked up Ryker's hand and held it in mine, just like I had in the ambulance. Tears flowed freely as I watched his chest rise and fall, the beeping of the machine telling me he was still alive.

An oxygen tube laced his face above his top lip, entering his nose. And all I could think about was how uncomfortable that thing was. My eyes scanned his features through the blur in my eyes. Ryker's head was covered in bandage, bloodstains cascaded down his temples past his ears to the dark blue bruises under his eyes. Surgical tape bound his flesh together on his cheek and his nose.

What did they do to you?

A knock at the door pulled me from my dulled state. Turning my head, I saw Mae and Dakin standing in the doorway, waiting for confirmation to enter.

"May we—" Mae started, but the words cut off as she lay eyes on Ryker.

I could tell she was holding back a sob as they entered the room after I nodded at them. "Thought you could use something to eat." She held up a takeaway bag from Big Al's.

I hadn't even thought about food, but the aroma that drifted through the room made my stomach growl. It had been hours since I'd had something to eat.

"How is he?" Mae asked as she handed me the bag.

"Still hasn't woken up yet, but the doctor said that it was normal for his type of injury," I replied, grimacing at the hoarseness of my voice. I opened the paper bag and saw the double cheeseburger and fries. I took a fry from the bag and chewed on it.

Taking out the burger, I unwrapped it from its paper covering and took a big bite. I could taste the sauces and the spice, but it tasted bland in my mouth. I took another bite and placed some fries in inside my mouth simultaneously, chewing the food like a chipmunk without actually tasting any of it. Before I knew it, the food was finished, and I felt sick to my stomach. I knew I needed it for energy, but stress knotted my insides, making me feel vulgar.

"Thank you," I said, as I threw the empty package into the small dustbin at the edge of the bed.

Mae just looked at me with sympathy as she nodded. Silence filled the room as we stared at Ryker lying peacefully on his bed, unaware of what was happening around him. A yawn crept up and before I could stop it, it came out like a loud yelp, tears glimmering around my vision.

"Maybe you should get some rest," Dakin said, placing a hand on my shoulders supportively.

"That's a great idea," Mae agreed, staring at me like a loving mother would.

"I'm fine," I lied as another yawn escaped me.

"You are not fine. You're tired. It's been a long day. Come, I'll take you home," Dakin said as an unfamiliar smile curved his lips.

"I don't want to leave Ryker," I snapped, lifting Ryker's hand into mine.

"I'll stay with him. Go. Let Dakin take you home. Get some rest and come back tomorrow," Mae offered as she started making Ryker more comfortable by fluffing his pillow and pulling the covers up higher.

I nodded my agreement as Dakin's hand slid under my arm, pulling me up.

I looked at him as I stood, his hand never leaving my arm. He smiled at me again with the strange look, and I knew that something was wrong. Dakin was never so forceful and hard. His features seemed unfamiliar to me as we started walking through the hospital. Glancing now and then to him, his face contorted periodically as if he was fighting something inside himself.

This was not the Dakin I knew.

CHAPTER 21

*D*akin guided me to the exit of the hospital. Guiding was a gentle term. No. Dakin was pulling me forcefully. Glancing up at him as we walked through the doors, I noticed his features were hard and tense. He was resigned as his jaw muscles tensed, jumping with every pulse as he seemed to gnaw on his teeth. Something was very wrong. I felt it in my bones.

It was as if the elements knew it, too. A wind picked up as we walked through the almost deserted parking lot to the truck. Lost raindrops fell on my cheek as if trying to warn me about something.

When we got to the truck, Dakin opened the door for me to get in, practically shoving me inside. The door slammed shut, and I jumped at the loud bang in the silence. We hadn't spoken a word since leaving Ryker's room. Usually Dakin would have said something to ease my worries.

He walked around the front of the truck, and I could see the lightness of his steps were gone. He used to bounce when he walked, almost as if enjoying life and every moment, but watching him now . . . it was like watching a person struggling with quicksand. The heaviness of his strides seemed to weigh him down. Almost as if he didn't know how to move. As if he didn't know how to be Dakin. Instincts nudged at me, but I couldn't understand what my gut was trying to tell me. Dakin started the vehicle, and we pulled out the parking lot, leaving the hospital in our rearview mirror.

"Thank you for taking me home, and for being there for me," I said softly, breaking the silence.

"Where else would I be?" Dakin replied, tapping my leg as he gave me a fake smile. His eyes shone an amber hue before changing back to the brilliant blue I was familiar with.

Was that a trick of the light? I was sure his eyes just changed color, but looking at him now, all I could see was the blue shining brightly with passing lights. Had I imagined it? I knew stress and fatigue could cause hallucinations, but this seemed too real to be a figment of my imagination. Something inside me screamed that what I was experiencing was the truth. That something was not right.

We neared the house, and I felt compelled to test Dakin, to make sure that it was still my friend.

"Thank you for the lake. I had fun, especially the kiss," I said, trying to sound sincere as I forced myself to grab hold of his hand.

"The kiss was the best part of the day," he replied, giving my hand a tight squeeze.

Chills ran down my spine. This wasn't my Dakin. This was someone else. We stopped in front of the house, and I unbuckled myself, opening the door in one swift motion. I muttered a "thank you" as I wanted to leave the truck to make my way toward the front door, seeing it as my only salvation. Dakin grabbed my wrist hard, forcing me to turn around.

"What's the rush?"

"It's been a long day. I need to get some rest," I replied, watching his hand tighten around me as another glimmer of amber shot across his irises. Pulling my hand free of his grip with more force than I needed, I left the truck, slamming the door behind me as I hurried to the house.

Just as I was about to step onto the porch, a firm hand grabbed my arm, hard. I yelped. Turning around, I faced Dakin. My breath vanished.

His features were hard as stone, his blue eyes now had an amber hue. This time there was no trick of the light that I could blame. A menacing smile spread across his face as his grip tightened around my wrist.

Instincts kicked in immediately as I used the move Ryker taught me for the same side wrist grab. I clasped my hands together as I stepped toward Dakin on the side. I lifted my elbow and broke the hold he had on me. Without thinking, I used the momentum of the swing and forced my elbow to his face, but he blocked me, swatting it away like it was nothing.

With unnatural speed, he spun me around, grabbing my head in a lock and cutting off some of my air supply. I could feel his breath on the side of my face as he whispered in my ear.

"Ryker taught you well. I'm impressed." Dakin's voice sounded wrong. Hoarse, as if it wasn't his own. I struggled against his grip as it tightened around my neck. "You have the same tenacity as Kaye and your mother had." I could hear the smile in his voice as bile rose in my throat. I stopped struggling at the shock of his words.

"If only my brother could see you now."

"Gorice," I gasped.

"Ah, so you have heard of me." Amusement crept into his voice as his grip on the chokehold eased a bit.

That was all I needed.

Without warning, I grabbed the arm around my neck and pulled forward. I swung my arm back, hitting him between the legs. The grip eased as I used it to my advantage. I stepped to the side, half turning so I could place my one leg behind his, and sat down on the ground, pulling him with me so he fell on his back. I hit him twice between the legs. Using his momentary pain, I got to my knees, then bent his arm up and behind his back, forcing him on his stomach. Twisting the arm to the side, I placed my knee on his shoulder blade, ready to break or dislocate the arm if needed.

"Give me one good reason why I shouldn't just kill you now?" I asked through clenched teeth as anger seared through me.

Laughing mockingly, Gorice spoke. "Whatever you do to me, you do to your familiar."

"Liar!" I shouted as I pulled on his arm more, digging my knee deeper into his shoulder. Wincing from the pain, he spoke through gritted teeth. "If I die, my brother will never wake up. His coma is magically induced." I eased up a little on the pressure as the words hit my reality. "It's a contingency plan." He laughed as I grunted in my frustration. I was certain he was lying, but I couldn't be sure. Part of me wanted to kill him right then, but if he was telling the truth, I couldn't risk it.

"What do you want?"

"If you will let me up so we can discuss it like civilized beings, then I will tell you."

"There is nothing civilized about you. There is nothing civilized about possessing my friend."

"Oh, come now . . . you and I are more alike than you think."

Anger seeped through me, and all I wanted to do was beat the living shit out of him, but that would mean hurting Dakin. Reluctantly, I let go of Gorice and jumped back a few steps, my eyes never leaving him. He got up and dusted the ground from his clothes.

"It's so much better possessing a being that you know. That you care about," Gorice said mockingly with arrogance in his voice.

"What do you want?" I asked again, sending daggers at him with my eyes, ready to knock him down again if he tried something.

"Isn't it obvious, my little hidden one? I want your soul."

I smirked. "Not for sale. How did you find me?"

"I have my ways. Power like yours shines a light that can even be seen even in the ethereal."

Like that wasn't a bullshit answer. I rolled my eyes, waiting for him to get to the point.

How was I going to get rid of him and save Dakin?

I looked around, trying to find something to fight with, but there wasn't a weapon in sight.

"It's no use, little one. No one will be able to save you, but I'm not here to harm you. Yet."

"If you want my soul so bad, why don't you just take it?" I asked as I mirrored his steps with every move, keeping the distance between us.

A smile tugged at his lips as he watched me with curiosity.

"My dear, did my brother not tell you? With soul-transfer spells, the *participant*"—he gestured toward me, emphasizing the word—"must be willing. If I force the life out of you, it would not work. I need you to give it to me of your own free will."

"Yeah, not gonna happen," I bit back, an acidic taste filling my mouth at the mere thought of it.

"That is actually a damn shame. Maybe there is a way I can *persuade* you to give it to me?" He moved to his right, and I mimicked his movements. Then he moved to the left, and I did the same. There was no way I was going to let him out of my sight. Without waiting for an answer or a retort from me, he managed to dislocate Dakin's shoulder.

Gorice winced in pain and muttered a curse under his breath, but he straightened up again, the blue of Dakin's eyes fading back to the amber I had now begun associated with this monster. I wanted to help my friend, but I didn't want to get near this SOB.

"Still nothing? Why, Amunet, I'm shocked that you would allow your friend to be in so much pain. Maybe an arm would change your mind." Before I could stop him, he broke Dakin's arm.

I heard the crack of the bone and Gorice screamed in pain, falling to his knees as he clutched the arm that was now rendered useless.

Dakin's eyes shone through the amber, and I could see the pain in his eyes—the real eyes of my best friend. Tears welled in my eyes. There was nothing I could do! I wanted to help, but how? I looked around, but it was as if all the nosy neighbors were all fast asleep and no one heard a peep. Maybe Gorice had dulled the sounds coming from my house?

"Stop it," I whispered. I didn't want Dakin to experience more pain.

A laugh sounded through the pain as the blue faded to amber again and Gorice made his appearance.

"Maybe . . ." He winced as he got up. "Maybe I should cause more pain and try a leg?" Gorice moved and angled the leg in front of him.

Before I could even think, I spoke. "Stop!" Tears glimmered in my eyes and fell to the floor as I dropped my gaze to the ground. "I'll do it."

"What was that? I couldn't quite hear you over the alignment of the stars," Gorice coaxed me with his words.

"I said I'll do it. Just spare Dakin any more pain. Please."

He straightened and walked toward me. His hands were rough and warm, but the touch felt cold as he wiped the tears from my face.

"I'm so happy that you have seen reason. It would have been a shame for your familiar to feel more pain. He is quite loud in here." He tapped his head, indicating that Dakin was still inside. "I tell you what. As a sign of good faith, I will give you two days. You know, to get your affairs in order and say your goodbyes. After the sun has set on the second day, you belong to me."

My head dropped as I choked back tears. A strong wind picked up and swooshed in front of me, throwing my tangled hair in my face. When it died down, I looked up, but I saw no one. Gorice had vanished. I turned around and saw Dakin's truck on the side of the road, but no sign of his body or the assbutt that had inhabited it.

What had I done?

CHAPTER 22

I stood on the grass for a while as everything started sinking in. Ryker's attack, the magically induced coma . . . that meant Gorice or one of his Tainted slobs had used magic to put him in a coma. Without thinking, I made my way to the house, opening the battered door and closing it behind me. The silence of the house was deafening. Usually, Ryker would be sitting in his armchair, drinking a tea he'd concocted in the kitchen and reading his newspaper, giving voice to his opinion on whatever he had just read.

I stared at the empty seat as I entered the room. I could see him sitting there, smiling at me as I took a seat on the long sofa. I could hear the kettle whistling in the kitchen, could even hear his voice as he asked me how my day had been. The image of him faded as I blinked back tears. His presence vanished as the destruction of what the Tainted had done took over the space that Ryker had once occupied.

Just thinking about the Tainted made the sadness disappear, sending blindingly white anger through my veins. Heat rose in me, and I felt my neck and face light up. My hands started tingling and shaking at the sight of the chaos littering the house.

This has to end. Now!

My scorching anger increased from the fiery pits of hell with every memory. First, they came after me. Attacked me on multiple occasions. They killed my mother, caused Kaye's death, then they attacked Ryker, and now the son of a bitch had the audacity to possess my best friend and try to coerce me into giving up my soul so an asshole can be reincarnated and destroy the light?

The rage inside threatened to explode. I wanted to punch something or someone. I wanted to cause so much pain that no one would ever think to fuck with me again. I picked up a vase from the table and threw it with all my might against the wall, sending shards of glass scattering throughout the space. Some of my anger left me as the vase hit the wall.

I picked up a broken photo frame and threw it against the wall. I kicked at the broken wood littering the floor. The scatter pillows flew throughout the room as I took what I could find just to get rid of the hatred boiling inside me.

When I didn't have the energy to throw or break another thing, I let out a scream of anguish and frustration as I slid down the wall, letting my head fall between my knees. I was spent. All the emotions came to the surface, and I welcomed them, letting the screams out into the night.

My sobs died down as exhaustion overtook me. It was all I had left inside of me. I closed my eyes, not even having the energy to move as I waited for sleep to claim me.

I heard the echo of a voice, and I forgot where I was. My eyes flew open. It could have easily been my imagination with the lack of sleep, but when I heard it again, I thought it was Mae come to check on me. But at this time of night? Why wouldn't she just let herself in? My thoughts went to the Tainted, and I jumped up, looking for something I could use as a weapon. I grabbed a fire poker and walked to the window to see if someone was outside.

I didn't get far when I heard the voice again. It sounded like it was coming from behind me. I turned around, only to be greeted with the darkness and a broken lamp flickering on the floor.

I was alone.

Just the thought of that sent a bolt of fear to my chest. I didn't have the energy or even the bravado to deal with an intruder. Not now.

Amunet.

"Who's there?" I yelled at no one.

Silence.

"I swear I will kill whoever is hiding in this house. Come out now!" I screamed. I didn't know if I wanted someone to come out or not.

Amunet.

The voice seemed to be all around me. I turned, trying to sense anything, to see a shadow lurking in the dark hallways, but there was nothing. The only crazy person around was me.

Suddenly, the fireplace roared to life, lighting the room in a glow of summer bonfires. I yelped in fright as I dropped the poker, jumping back and tumbling over a side table. I landed on something concrete, but I couldn't take my eyes off the blazing fire.

"Who are you? What do you want?" I asked, looking for someone that wasn't there. Was it a fire fae that had come to play? Did they even exist? I didn't know and frankly didn't care. This shit wasn't normal.

See.

I could now make it out as a woman's voice. See? What was I supposed to see? What did this spirit want from me?

See.

I looked around, hoping to find something that would give me the answers. As my vision danced across the room, I thought I saw something in the corner next to the fireplace, but when my gaze went back there, there was nothing. Only a shimmer.

Hidden magic, I thought as I remembered what Ryker had said about the shimmers. Crawling on my hands and knees, I made my way to the corner, keeping an eye on the fire, as if it was more alive than normal. Sure enough, a shimmer sparkled in the faint light. I waved my hand over the spot and recited the words Ryker had taught me to make the hidden seen. The shimmer faded, and the grimoire stood in its place. Ryker must have hidden it when the Tainted arrived.

I took the heavy book and placed it on the coffee table in front of the fireplace. I paged through the book, but I saw nothing. What was I supposed to do? I looked at the fire, not knowing how to talk to it.

Feeling foolish, I asked, "What do you want me to do?"

A powerful gust of wind blew around me. The pages of the grimoire moved, and as suddenly as it started, the wind stopped at a page that I hadn't paid attention to earlier. I read the title and looked at the fire.

"*To summon a spirit*. You want me to do this spell?" The flames increased in height and intensity. I took that as a yes.

I needed the elements for the casting of the circle, as well as salt. I stood and pushed the table to the side of the room, making space for the circle. I moved to the kitchen for the ingredients I needed.

I took four bowls from the cabinets and looked around for the elements I could place inside. Turning around and rummaging through the kitchen, my eyes fell on the pool of blood on the floor. It was crusting around the edges as it started drying, and a feeling of guilt and sadness overwhelmed me.

Ryker.

Just the thought of him brought tears to my eyes. Seeing him lying on the floor, covered in blood, barely breathing . . . I struggled to hold back a whimper. Blinking back my tears, the image of him on the floor faded and I was left clutching the bowls, staring at an empty floor covered with the remnants of the events that took place.

Taking a breath to steady myself, I continued my search for the elements and filled the bowls—one for water; for air, I grabbed incense; for earth, I took the crystals that stood in the window; for fire, I took a candle.

I took the components back to the living room, the fire still burning in the hearth, then I set the elements in their respective directions. As I set each component down, I recited the elemental invocation that would seal the circle.

"Earth, Air, Fire, and Water, open your hands to me. Earth, Air, Fire, and Water, open your spirit to me. Earth, Air, Fire, and Water, open your energy to me. Earth, Air, Fire, and Water, lend your power to me."

The circle was complete as I placed the last ingredient down in its direction. The water started bubbling as if it was boiling. The incense started smoking. The crystals glowed and the candle lit itself. Acknowledging that I didn't do such a crappy job, I made my way to the table where I'd left the grimoire. Picking up the book, I took a few steps away from the circle, still wary of what might actually come through with the spell. I took a deep breath to steady myself and calm my nerves.

"Hear these words, hear my cries, spirits from the other side. Come to me, I summon thee. Cross now the great divide."

Wind swirled around the room. I looked around. There were no open windows or doors. The circle sparked to life, causing its own light to shine, connecting the elements in a visible line. The sparkling embers of the fire twirled with the shimmers of the circle. The colors dancing around the circle mesmerized me. Not one spark left where it all started swirling around in the center. At first, it was just at the bottom of the floor, but when an image started forming, the embers and sparks drifted up, highlighting the feet of a woman. As it traveled up, the body started taking shape. The legs, covered in a layer of white material shimmering through the flames. Next, the middle and hands started forming, and I could see that the dress the woman was wearing had long sleeves, coming together in a sharp V-shape at the middle finger. Reddish-brown curls hung around her shoulders, cascading down to her middle.

Time seemed to speed up and slow down simultaneously as the features of the face came into view. A long, sharp chin, full lips, cheekbones to die for, and blue-gray eyes that stared right into my soul with no judgment. The face seemed familiar, like I'd met this woman before and couldn't remember it.

"Amunet." Her voice sounded like angels sighing, beautiful and full of love. "My beautiful granddaughter." She lifted her arms in my direction.

"Kaye."

CHAPTER 23

This couldn't be happening. How was this even possible?

I knew I could do great things with the power that I had, but how in the world could I have conjured up this? I must have been hallucinating. Kaye was here, standing right in front of me as if she had never died four hundred years ago. Her reddish-brown hair cascaded in curls over her shoulders, coming to rest at her waist. Her gentle blue-gray eyes shimmered in the dimly lit room as her full lips curved into a smile.

I stared at her. "Is this real?"

Her omnipresence could be felt all around the room as if she brought life to the chaos in the house.

"It is as real as the magic in your soul." Kaye laughed, and it sounded like bell chimes. She opened her arms and gestured for me to come closer. Without even thinking about it, I crossed the threshold of the circle and stepped into her arms. Her embrace was as warm as the sunlight on a summer's day. She held me tight, stroking my hair and planting a kiss on my head. Closing my eyes, I took everything in. She smelled like early morning dew mixed with roses and lavender. Her caress felt so warm and caring, like that of a mother. Ryker had done a great job at raising me and comforting me when I was upset, but nothing could compare to the embrace of a mother.

The thought of Ryker made my throat close with emotions.

"What's weighing so heavily on your heart, my little light?" Kaye asked as her embrace around me tightened.

All my emotions boiled up to the surface. Unable to control myself, I started crying. Kaye stroked my hair softly, and she whispered reassuring words into my ears. She led me to the sofa, and we sat down, her arms never leaving my shoulders.

"Let me look at you." She scooted away from me slightly, holding me at arm's length. Her gaze roamed over me. "You are even more beautiful than I had seen. And you were amazing in my visions. Beautiful, strong, caring with a hint of mischief, just like your mother."

I stared at her in shock. How did she know all of that? I remember Ryker had said that she had a vision of her future, but I didn't think that it had included me. Kaye's eyes showed nothing but calm.

"Now tell me, Amunet, what has you so troubled? What is causing those wise eyes to cry?"

"Where to begin?" I asked as I wiped the tears from my face. Taking a deep breath, I started telling her everything—the attack from the Tainted, which unlocked my magic; how Ryker had explained everything to me and trained me; how my friends were spies and how I felt betrayed by it all; how Ryker was attacked and put into a magical coma; and how Gorice had possessed my best friend who was supposed to be my familiar. I ended with what had happened a few hours earlier when Gorice said he wanted my soul. When I finished, it felt like a weight had been lifted off my shoulders and I could breathe again. We sat there in silence, and I knew Kaye was digesting everything.

Her brow furrowed slightly. "I knew that the ethereal wouldn't have been enough. Gorice has such a dark heart and so much unfinished business that he was trapped in his own time loop of his death. I had hoped he wouldn't be able to escape, but clearly, he found a way around it." She paused, taking a deep breath, and shook her head as if to rid herself of the memories. Kaye looked up at me again with a gentle smile as she stroked my face gingerly. "Whatever happens, do not give in to Gorice or his minions. Giving into him would mean the end."

"I—" I started, not knowing how to voice the fear that had built within me. My gaze dropped from Kaye's to the floor. "I don't know if I will be able to resist. To fight." Traitorous tears fell from my eyes and I almost cursed. I'd thought I was out of tears.

"You are stronger than you think, my love." Kaye's hands lifted my face so I could look at her. The touch was soft and warm, emanating love as she spoke. "I know it's hard. I know your emotions are running rampant through you right now, but you cannot give in. You cannot let him win. Always think of the greater good, not just for you and the ones you love—but for everyone." She pulled me into her arms, holding me like a mother would her daughter after a heartbreak.

"I would have given anything to live a long and happy life with Ryker and Samena, but the greater good called for sacrifice, and I had to send Gorice to the ethereal. If I didn't, that long life I envisioned wouldn't have been that long." Kaye's words were a soft murmur as she stroked my hair, and I could hear the sadness in her voice.

We lay on the couch in silence, with Kaye comforting me, playing with my hair. It must have been awful for her to give up her life to save everyone else, knowing she'd never see her daughter grow up, and never be able to hold her husband and share intimate kisses under the stars again.

Would I have made the same choice as Kaye if I was in that situation? Would I have run with my family to a safe place? Would I have tried to fight? My mind went wild with all the possibilities, but the only thing I knew for certain was that Gorice had to be stopped no matter what.

"Kaye? What should I do?" I asked, turning my head slightly to look at her.

"That is a hard question, and an even harder situation. I cannot tell you what you should do, I can only give you advice. Even though it's hard, you should always take the small steps and do the next right thing. Sometimes you just need some clarity to know what the right thing is."

Clarity. I definitely needed that right now. The soothing motion of her stroking my hair calmed me so much that my eyes started drifting closed.

I had no idea how long I had been asleep before the visions started. First, there was nothing but darkness, and then swirling lights entered my vision. Whites, golds, blues, and greens swirled in front of me as if I was part of the *Barbie's The Nutcracker* movie. It started off soft, but soon the colors intensified, forming an image in front of me.

I heard sounds of rushing water and birds singing as the image started taking shape. Beautifully lush, green mountains came into view, accompanied by the most magnificent waterfall I had ever seen. It looked like something out of a fantasy film. Animals roamed the ground as the sky cleared into a brilliant blue, a rainbow shining bright as neon against the sky. The sun was warm against my skin. I was awestruck at the beauty.

Some sort of building started forming—no, not a building. A temple. As big as it was tall, covered in gold, the temple shimmered like the sun on a lake on a hot summer's day. There were no doors or windows, but instead there were hollowed-out openings where those things would have been. It had to be a dream, especially since the wild animals paid no attention to me. The predators walked about, mingling peacefully with what would have been their prey as if they were old friends.

The energy of this place was absolutely amazing. I hadn't felt that much at peace in forever. If this was the afterlife, I wouldn't mind staying here forever. Then it hit me. Was this the afterlife? Was I dead? The last thing I recalled was falling asleep on Kaye's lap.

"You are not dead, my child," a gentle, familiar voice came from behind me.

A scream caught in my throat as fear tightened my shoulders. I spun around, my gaze landing on a woman.

That wasn't right. This wasn't a normal woman. She seemed empowered. Magical. Powerful. Yet her face and features were soft, caring, motherly. She had dark, almost-black curly hair, which flowed down her back. A crown made up of vines and branches rested on top of her head. The light made her skin glow golden. Her eyes were a golden hue, large and round, and they seemed to look right into your soul. A smile spread across her long, oval face, making it shimmer. I was speechless at this woman standing in front of me, wearing nothing but a white tunic that hardly covered anything. The confidence that radiated off her was something else entirely.

"Who are you?" I asked, my voice barely above a whisper. I knew I'd seen her before, but I couldn't place the memory.

"I am Gaia, mother to all. And you are Amunet Wicc, born of Willows, the Hidden One."

"I met you before." I suddenly remember the goddess telling me to wake up when I was in the hospital. "How do you know who I am?"

"The women in your bloodline have always had a connection to me and the balance that my dragon and I bestow. You are the last of your line, and that makes you special." Gaia's smile radiated like the sky, the temple, and the rainbow combined. It felt like I had known her all my life, like a long-lost connection of my soul that I had only now found.

"Why am I here?" I looked around, gesturing vaguely around me. "What is this place?"

"This is the Sacred Temple of Balance. Some even call it the Temple of Gaia, but I am not only her. I am the balance of life, of love, of heaven and earth. You, my dear, have come here in search of clarity."

"Clarity?"

"Yes, clarity. Your world is resting on a double-edged sword right now. One wrong move and the balance will be tipped. You have asked for clarity in maintaining the balance so your world would not end in darkness."

I was confused. How did I end up here? How was this even possible? If I wasn't dead, was I dreaming?

"I have so many questions. Too many, really," I said, feeling sheepish about my train of thought.

Gaia lifted my chin, forcing me to look at her. She radiated so much power that it was difficult to look at her, but I couldn't take my gaze off her.

"Let us take a walk, my child. I find the spring near the waterfall quite soothing in times of confusion." She placed her hand at the back of my shoulder, leading me to the wondrous nature of the waterfall. As we walked, I noticed that it wasn't just wild animals roaming the grounds, but the creatures from myths and legends.

Horses mingled with centaurs, birds shared the sky with dragons, and what I assumed were fireflies were dancing with fairies. Nothing about this place made any sense.

"How do these creatures exist?" I asked, gesturing to the fae, centaurs, and dragons.

"They have always existed. At one time, these beings existed in your world, but when humanity became a threat to them, they sought shelter in the other realms. That is why they are only the things in stories for you. It was either that or risk the balance of magic."

It made sense. I remember reading that the fae had gone into hiding at the coming of the Iron Age, but I thought it was only old wives' tales . . . until now.

We stopped at the small spring that was fed from the waterfall. The water was crystal clear, surrounded by rocks and gemstones scattered across the shoreline. I heard music—singing, to be exact—but I didn't see anyone. I looked up at Gaia, wanting to ask her where it was coming from. She smiled at me, nodding to the water. I turned my gaze back to the pool and watched. The water rippled about and mermaids broke through the surface. Their tails glimmered as they climbed on the rocks, bathing in the sun. Their song became louder and hypnotic. I could sit there and watch them all day. But when Gaia touched my shoulder, she pulled me from the trance of the merfolk's magic.

"They are something to behold, aren't they?"

"They definitely are. I can't believe this is all real. It feels like a dream," I whispered, my eyes locked on the merfolk.

"You are definitely dreaming, but that doesn't make it any less real. How else are you here?"

I frowned at Gaia.

"What do you mean?"

"Even though you are gifted by the gods, you are still, in a way, human. Your magic, the ether in your soul, grants you passage to this realm through projection. Your body is still resting at home, but your mind and soul are here . . . temporarily, of course."

I nodded in understanding. I vaguely remembered reading about astral projection in the grimoire. I'd wanted to ask Ryker about it, but never had the time. Thinking about him reminded me of why I was here . . . if that was even the reason I was here.

"Gaia, I don't know what to do. You said I was here for clarity, but I'm still as confused as ever." I stared up at the goddess, hoping to find the answers I needed.

She sat down on one of the rocks at the pool, dipping her feet into the shallow waters and gesturing for me to do the same.

"The thing with humans is that they tend to overthink everything." She smiled, kicking the water. "What would keep the balance is, well, keeping the balance. That would be for the good of all. Sometimes sacrifices need to be made to keep it as such, but they are for the light and dark to co-exist in harmony. What do you think would restore the balance?" she asked, leaning back on her hands to soak up the sun.

I thought about her words, and the goddess let me. There was still balance in the world, but it was as frail as an unraveling thread. That had to be because Gorice had escaped from the ethereal. To keep the balance, Gorice should return to the ethereal. The Tainted should be stopped at any cost.

"There is your answer," Gaia said as if she'd heard my thoughts.

Just as I was about to ask her more, I woke on the couch in my living room.

CHAPTER 24

I stood in front of the hospital doors, bracing myself to go see Ryker. He hadn't woken up yet, but now I knew why. Gorice still had a hold on him, but that was about to change.

As I walked through the doors, my breathing hitched with the noxious scent of disinfection and floor polish. Patients loitered in the hallways, and doctors as nurses bounced through the rooms, helping where they could, carting charts to and from each room.

I made my way to the elevator, trying to avoid everyone milling around as I tugged the straps of the backpack higher on my shoulder. The weight of the contents felt heavier with every step, even though they weighed almost nothing. But their intentions sat like boulders on my shoulders. The elevator dinged, and the doors slid open. I stepped aside to let the people out and slipped inside before the door could close.

As I pressed the button for the third floor, I thought about the morning before, when I'd woken from my dream about Gaia.

I'd jolted awake, startled and out of sorts. It had taken me a moment to figure out where I was. Sunlight seeped through the windows, cascading golden light into the living room. Stretching out, my feet hooked the blanket covering me. I couldn't remember even falling asleep. I looked around, but the room seemed normal. Nothing was out of place, which in itself seemed out of place.

The space was clean. Everything was back in their original places. All that was missing was a couple of the dining room chairs and the paintings and portraits that had been broken.

"Hello?" I asked, not really expecting a reply.

"Morning, honey. I hope you had a wonderful sleep." Kaye came out from the kitchen, a drying cloth on one hand and a teacup in the other. "Hope you're hungry. I'm making breakfast." She smiled before heading back to the kitchen. Shock coursed through me, and then I recalled summoning my grandmother's spirit.

I got up and trotted off, following the scent of coffee and baked goods. My stomach grumbled as I sank onto a chair. The kitchen was as clean as the rest of the house. My gaze drifted to where I knew damage used to be, but nothing was broken. Everything was in its place and spotless. Kaye placed a cup in front of me and glanced at the spot.

"I hope you don't mind. The house was a mess, and you were sleeping so soundly. Spirits don't sleep, so I thought I might bide my time with something useful."

"I appreciate it. Don't know if I would have had the mental capacity to do it myself." I took a sip of the coffee, waiting for the slow burn of the bitter nectar, but nothing came. The liquid was warm, but there was no bitterness. There was a floral fragrance that simmered through, along with a smooth vanilla taste. It still tasted like coffee, but better.

"What is this?" I closed my eyes and sniffed at the sweet floral scent I held in my hand.

"Oh, just a remedy I used to make way back when. It has all the benefits of tea with the added kick you need in that caffeine stuff you drink."

"You need to share the recipe, it's delish." I took another sip and relished the taste.

Kaye laughed and turned as the oven pinged. As she opened it, the aroma hit me harder than the drink. She placed a tray filled with muffins on the counter.

"You baked? I think you should move in."

"Ryker was never one for cooking. He knows how to survive, but I won't really call his food cooking."

I laughed at her statement, nearly spitting out my drink.

"Don't tell him I said that. Then again, maybe you should tell him I said that. Maybe he would stop being so lazy and actually make something decent for you."

I laughed even harder as she joined in. Picking up a muffin, I took a bite and felt like I was in heaven. "Holy crap!"

"Language!" Kaye scolded playfully.

"Sorry, but this is absolutely amazing. What's in this?"

"Oh, another Willows' magic recipe. I'll write it down for you before I leave."

I choked on my bite, suddenly filled with dread. I didn't want to be alone. Not now.

"Why do you have to go?"

"Oh, sweetie, the magic only lasts for twenty-four hours." She came over and pulled me into a hug as tears formed. I was just getting to know her, and now she was leaving. It felt like I was being left behind. There was so much I wanted to do with her, to know about her. I needed her help with Ryker and Gorice. Gaia had given me the answer, but I still needed Kaye's help.

~

*T*he elevator dinged, pulling me out of my memories. When the doors slid open, the busy hallways greeted me. I walked toward the nurses' station and stopped a few feet short. What was I going to say? I wanted to know if there was any update on him, even though I already knew nothing had changed, but there was still that inkling of hope that something might have changed.

"Morning, hun. Can I help you?" an older nurse came to stand next to me, her gray hair cut into a short pixie style, brown eyes creased with age but held empathy in their shine. Her lips curved into laughing lines stained with a light pink lipstick that didn't really match her skin tone.

"Morning. I, uh, I was just wondering . . ." I felt silly. I could have just gone past to Ryker's room, but I was delaying. I didn't think I was ready to do what I had to do.

"Oh, I remember you. Wicc, right? Ryker Wicc's niece. Oh, he will be so happy to see you."

"He would?" I didn't know what hit me first. Shock. Relief. Something I couldn't name.

"Yes, he would. Now, he hasn't woken up yet, but I just know he can hear everything around him. He even has a few admirers." She giggled as she gestured for me to follow her down the hall.

"He has?"

"Oh yes, he does. Your uncle is a very attractive man, so many nurses have taken to him. I had to chase four of them out of his room yesterday." She laughed as she nodded to four younger nurses on the side, standing across the doorway of Ryker's room, giggling like schoolgirls. A smile spread across my face at the mere thought of Ryker having a following. We stopped at the door and the head nurse showed me inside, following me.

She started checking his vitals and marking them down on his chart as I sat down on the chair next to Ryker's bedside. She squeezed my shoulder gently.

"I'll be outside if you need anything. Take your time."

I nodded my thanks, and she left, her white sneakers squeaking on the tiles.

"What are you doing here? Get back to work, you can drool later."

I looked over my shoulder through the window into the hall, watching the group of admirers scatter as the head nurse scolded them. I laughed at the sight, but as I turned back to Ryker, my smile faded.

He looked worse. The bruises on his face had darkened while some had started to heal, causing shades of blue and purple to change into a greenish yellow. It looked so painful. I grabbed his hand in mine and held it tight.

"Looks like you have some stalkers. Going to have your hands full when you get out of here." I kept quiet for a while, as if expecting him to protest, to tell me he had no idea what I was talking about. Just thinking about him and how he would react to the attention from the nurses had me smiling again.

"I miss you. I wish you were awake so you could tell me what I'm about to do is a stupid idea and that I'm going to get myself killed. To scold me and send me to my room. Anything would be better than this silence." I let go of his hand, then opened my backpack. Rummaging through it, I pulled out the clear quartz crystal staff Kaye had suggested I bring. I placed it into Ryker's hand, curling his fingers around the coolness of the crystal. Closing my eyes, I could see the energy fields of the quartz running through Ryker's body. As I held his hand, I whispered the spell Kaye had suggested I use. It was a variation on the undoing spell in the grimoire. She said that it might take a while, but it would undo whatever Gorice had placed on Ryker.

"So much has happened in the last few days. I don't even know where to begin," I started telling him what had happened after I left the hospital and how I'd noticed Dakin wasn't himself. I told Ryker everything—the ultimatum Gorice had given me, me calling upon Kaye, and how much she had helped me in the last twenty-four hours.

"I can see why you loved her and why you still love her. She is absolutely amazing. She taught me a lot in the short time she was here." I dabbed away the tear that escaped as my mind drifted back to the goodbye I had shared with Kaye last night. I had only known her for one day, but she had already felt like family. Like a grandmother. Like a part of me.

"I know now what to do. How to end this once and for all. If I don't —" my throat got choked up with emotion, so I took a deep breath to steady myself. "If I don't make it home, just know that I love you. You have been the best father I could have ever wanted." I stood kissed Ryker on the forehead. I closed my blurry eyes, letting the tears fall. Without another word, I grabbed the bag and left the room. If I didn't leave right then, I might never leave. I might just curl up on the bed next to Ryker and forget about everything. I might just chicken out of everything, but then what would good would that do? Gorice would win.

As I walked through the hallways toward the exit, I called up a cab. I didn't make eye contact with anyone, not wanting to see the looks of concern on everyone's faces. I might just look into a face that would make me stop what I planned to do. I couldn't risk it. This world couldn't afford me not going through with the plan.

Once outside and in the cab, the nerves started pulling at my insides. I felt like puking, but my stomach was too knotted. Resting my head against the window, I closed my eyes, trying to steady myself, willing every inch of my body to be in sync with my mind and my soul. I gave the address to the driver and sank back into the seat.

I wanted to call Mae and tell her where I would be, but she would either talk me out of it or come and find me, which would put her in danger, and I couldn't risk that. The drive seemed to take forever, but not long enough when the driver woke me. I paid him and got out of the car. The less I talked to people, the better.

Watching the car drive off, I pulled out a map from the bag and looked at the red circle I'd drawn on it. Kaye had shown me how to scry for someone—locating a person using only their name or magical imprint. I'd made sure to have the driver drop me off a few blocks from the location, because I didn't want to alert the Tainted to my presence before I was ready.

I looked at my phone, checking the map and photos I'd googled after finding the location. I smiled to myself, remembering Kaye's glee and astonishment. She'd never seen how the internet worked. She had told me that by checking in from time to time, she had figured out some appliances like the stove and plumbing, but that computers were another marvel she'd yet to experience.

The look on her face when I'd typed in the address and showed her the street view on Google Maps had been hilarious. She'd commented that if they had this technology in the past, things would definitely have been different for them. I reassured her that the things of today aren't always as wonderful as it seemed. Yes, we had advancements that made life easier, we also had too much information, which caused a lot of division amongst the people. People were too sensitive about every-thing, and they spread hate and negativity like butter on toast. The media chose what to show to everyone, which was usually fear-led propaganda that just made everything worse. It was a vicious cycle that no one wanted to get out of—or more likely couldn't.

I switched off my phone and headed to the small hill at the end of the road. The Tainted would be waiting just beyond it, and I needed to be ready. I took out a couple of hex bags Kaye had helped me prepare with a spell made up with only my intentions. She'd said I would be able to create my own spells with the correct intentions and had showed me how. I just hoped it worked. I hid the bags inside my hoodie pockets, then muttered the spell that would render me invisible as I trudged over the hill toward the factory where Gorice would be waiting.

CHAPTER 25

$\mathcal{E}$ven though I was invisible, I still crouched and hid. It was possible that the Tainted would be able to see beyond the spell like Ryker had taught me, so I didn't want to risk it. I had no backup plan if the Tainted were able to see the unseen, so this had to work.

The abandoned factory seemed empty from afar, except for a few men walking around the perimeter. They had to be Gorice's Tainted goons—why else would anyone protect an empty factory? They were all dressed in black and sporting weapons. Some carried guns strapped to their hips and thighs, while others carried swords, blades, and batons. They clearly didn't take any shit when it came to security.

It seemed strange that so many of the Tainted were armed, but then I remember Ryker telling me that not all Tainted were gifted in the magical department. Not all of them had the power to take me on magically, but they sure as hell knew how to throw a punch, so I had to be careful. I wouldn't be able to take them all on simultaneously.

Moving in closer, I noticed two of the goons patrolling the entrance to the factory, so I ducked down behind one of the small containers. I positioned myself in order to watch their movements and spot the best opportunity to get past them, but after a few minutes, I knew it wouldn't be a straightforward task—especially if the spell didn't last.

I placed one of the hex bags by the container. It could serve as a distraction if needed. I hurried to the other side of the container, hoping I could get a better vantage point for an entry that way, but that wasn't the case at all. The only thing that changed was the view. I needed a distraction to lure the guards away and sneak in. I glanced about me, but the only thing I found were stones.

Here goes nothing.

I picked up a few rocks and lugged them at the guard. The first stone hit the one on the shoulder and he just brushed it off as if it was a bug. The next rock hit him harder in the same spot.

"Hey! Why'd you do that?" He turned toward the other guard, shooting daggers at him with his glare.

"Do what?"

"You threw something at me."

"I did no such thing. You must have been in the sun too long, mate. You're imagining things."

The second guard sounded as if he was an Australian with his accent and his casual use of the word 'mate' while the first one sounded more mid-west, but I could have been mistaken. I chucked the third stone at the Aussie guard and ducked, just in case. I felt like a naughty child doing something she wasn't supposed to do.

"Listen here, mate, just because you imagine things doesn't mean you can throw things at me," the Aussie snapped, rubbing at his head.

I stifled my giggle.

"What are you babbling about? I did no such thing."

"Oh, so you making me a liar, then?"

"Well, if the shoe fits."

I threw another stone, but my foot slipped, and I ended up tossing the rock in another direction completely. It clanked as it hit the pipes to the side of the factory. The bickering stopped.

This could easily go wrong.

"What was that?"

"Better go check it out, aye."

I watched as they moved off to the side, guns at the ready. This was it. My only shot. It was now or never. Getting to my feet, I made a run for the hangar door without a single glance at the guards. The gravel crunched so loud beneath my feet that it sounded like a glass store being bulldozed. With every step, I winced at the sound and cursed under my breath.

Once through the enormous doors, I ducked behind one of the closest machines, which happened to have a conveyor belt lining the way from the big steel casing. Making sure I was out of sight, I crouched there until my breathing regained some of its normalcy even though my heart still pounded in my ears. I hoped I was the only one that was hearing it. I heard the two guards from the outside coming back to their position at the entrance, and though I know they wouldn't be able to see or hear me, I still sucked in my breath, holding it until I knew I was in the clear.

"I swear, mate, I heard something on the ground," the Australian guy said as he took up his place again.

"Now look who's been in the sun too long. There was nothing."

"Of course, there was something. How else would you describe the sound of something walking on the gravel?"

"Maybe because we were the ones walking on it?"

The two of them kept bickering. If they were Gorice's best, then I had no reason to fear these idiots. Rolling my eyes, I turned away from the main door and scoped out the factory's interior.

It wasn't big, housing equipment and machinery to the side of the space, all interconnected with conveyors and control panels that seemed ancient in today's standards. The remnants of what once ran the production were covered in thick layers of grimes and dust. An abandoned forklift gathered dust in an open space on the other side. That must have been the space for man-operated machinery and workers to move in and out of the factory. There were offices at the back with boxes stacked against the walls. A door separated two large windows while at the edge of the wall a metal staircase led to a walkway running along the wall, cradling more windows surrounding a big double door.

There seemed to be lots of movement in those offices, so my suspicions told me I would probably find Gorice there. I just needed to get there without being detected, and somehow manage to get the Tainted out of the factory. Even though I was invisible, the odds of not being found out by all the Tainted here were not in my favor. I needed a distraction.

As I made my way to the back hall of the factory, I placed hex bags between the machinery. I had no idea how powerful the explosions would be, but at least it would serve as diversions. I hoped.

At the wall of the office, I hid behind some of the boxes, trying to peek inside the room and come up with a plan of action. Tainted moved about as if the room served as a cloning clinic and they were just spewing out more and more idiots. It was not what I had envisioned, but I was too far into the plan to back out now.

I concentrated on the hex bags I had placed outside, letting the magic know my intent of only setting them off as I muttered the spell. I felt the familiar tingle of magic being called up, stirring around my intentions as it stripped me of my invisibility and headed toward the hex bags outside.

Shit.

I hadn't thought that the doing magic would cause me to lose the unseen. Ryker had mentioned that it took practice to hold on to more than one spell at a time without losing the power of any of them. I didn't think it through, though. I tried to get the spell back, but I was drained. My magic didn't want to obey, and my stress levels were skyrocketing.

A few breaths later, an explosion sounded outside, shaking the ground and grabbing everyone's attention. Dust hung in the air as Tainted stormed out of the rooms, weapons at the ready, running to the open hangar door.

As the footsteps rushed away from me, I snuck out of the hiding place and hurried to the staircase, my eyes glued in front of me. My only purpose was to get to Gorice, do a depossession spell, and get Dakin back. I must have been too far gone in my head because without even seeing it coming, the bottom door swung open and two Tainted came out, shock clear on their faces as their eyes locked on mine.

Crap.

CHAPTER 26

The two Tainted stood frozen for a few seconds before their shock twisted into pure hate. One pulled out a baton and tapped it twice on his hand, a sadistic smile twisting his lips.

He came at me, baton at the ready, swinging it wildly through the air. I managed to dodge the first two swings by jumping out of the way, my eyes never straying from the second guy in my peripheral, as I didn't know when he might decide to jump into the fight. The third swing came from high above, and I used the opening to my advantage.

As he swung his arm down, I stepped into his space and saw the surprise shadowing his features. He had not expected me to do that. Raising my arm, I caught the baton in mid-swing. The sting from the assault burned, but I didn't let it show. Using the arm that caught the baton, I swung it down, making sure my arm was always in contact with the weapon, and brought it to the center of my body. Adjusting my body slightly, I slipped my hands down towards my assailant's hand. Using the move Ryker had drilled into me so many times, I bent over the pipe-like weapon, forcing the attacker to release it into my awaiting hands.

Still holding onto his arm, I took the baton and swung it with a backhand against his head while bending the arm. A loud thud sounded as it made contact with the skull. But I didn't stop. Using the motion, I swung forward with such force that when the black hardened plastic made contact with his nose, an instant crack suggested the nose had been broken. The Tainted screamed in pain as he flew backwards, splattering blood all over. I stuck out my leg as I shoved him to ground. He landed hard, his head hitting the cold cement floor. I struck the baton against his face again, making sure that he would not be getting up soon.

Arms wrapped around me from behind, knocking the weapon out of my hands. From what I could remember from this guy's appearance, he wasn't big. I squirmed a bit, testing the grip before throwing myself forward and immediately back, catching him off guard and knocking my head into his face. I didn't hear any bones break, unfortunately, but the grip loosened around me, and I staggered out of his reach. Black spots danced across my vision, telling me that if it had been any harder, I might have knocked myself out.

I shook my head, trying to get my focus back before the attacker came to his senses. About the same time that I recovered, so did the Tainted. He looked pissed. He ran towards me, with a scream of rage. As he neared, I sidestepped quickly, hunching down as I twisted around, throwing my leg out. It hurt like hell as my leg contacted his shins, sending him flailing forward, hitting the ground face first. I didn't think; I reacted. As he laid sprawled out on the floor, I jumped on his back, grabbed a hand full of his hair and pulled his head up enough so that I could hook my arm underneath. My right arm snaked around his throat, and I grabbed my left arm, forming the perfect chokehold. The Tainted struggled beneath me, so I increased the pressure of the hold. The more he fought, the harder I choked. His nails dug into my arms, trying to get a grip on me so I could release him. It burned like fire, but I couldn't give it my attention. My life depended on him going down.

After a few more wild struggles, the guy stopped moving. I released his head, and it hit the concrete with a thud. My breath came out in rough pants. I stood over the two unconscious bodies for a moment, staring but not really taking in anything when a noise ripped me from my reverie.

"Hey, you!" I turned and saw Tainted storming into the factory. I could only imagine how it looked from their point of view. This small teenager standing over the bodies of two of their unconscious brothers. I didn't blame them when they pulled out their weapons and started firing the at me.

Shots echoed through the factory as I dived behind one of the big metal machines. The loud clanking of metal on metal screamed through my ears.

What the hell was I going to do? This scenario hadn't even crossed my mind when I'd planned this out. How the hell was I going to fight against bullets?

I tried moving to another spot, but the bullets whizzed by my head, and I immediately ducked back to my position. This was impossible. More shouts echoed over the sound of rapidly repeating fire. They were going to get to me. It was inevitable. I tried once more to move to a different location, only to be caught short by a flying dagger heading my way. I dived underneath a conveyor, and it clipped the side of my face, drawing blood. The burn of the cut blistered on my cheek and the first knee-jerk reaction I had was to touch it.

I winced, drawing my fingers back from my face. They came away covered in blood. Helpless and hopeless, I felt like crying, but crying never fixed anything of this magnitude. A whimper escaped me as I stared up from underneath the conveyor.

Tucked away in the corner was one of the hex bags I had stashed. If I remembered correctly, I had at least three hidden between the machines. This would be my only shot to get to Dakin. I would have to wing it afterwards.

If I even made it that far.

The gunshots started dying down, but the shuffling of movements never did. From where I was hiding, I could make out the feet of the Tainted roaming about, probably getting hand queues from the leader. If I activated these bombs, I needed to be well away from here, but the place was crowded with Gorice's pawns with no way for me to get away. The only thing I could think of that could get me out of this predicament was to let it go off in succession.

I needed to time this right, otherwise I would blow my own head off. Before I set my intention on my magic, I looked at my only escape option after the first explosion went off. If everything happened as I hoped it would, the first explosion would cause chaos and clear the way to the staircase. I could run up there as fast as I could and try to miss the damage that would rain down on the factory.

"Here goes nothing," I whispered as I got ready to run. I closed my eyes and set my intention to what I wanted the magic to do. Once it was locked in, I whispered the spell and felt the magic leave my body. I could sense the energy travel along to the first hex bag. A golden-white light enveloped the bag, activating the ingredients in it, and the first bang sounded.

As I suspected, chaos erupted. People screamed and yelled at each other. Their attention focused in on the corner of the factory near the door as metal and wood splinters cascaded through the air. I didn't know whether it was a delayed reaction to the blast, but I could have sworn I'd heard gunshots as well.

I got out from under the machine and ran toward the stairway, but my pants got snagged on the edge of protruding metal.

Shit!

I yanked and pulled, but the fabric didn't want to give. The metal wouldn't give, nor would the pants rip. This was not good. Within a few seconds, the other explosions would be activated, and I would be done for. I pulled as hard as I could, watching the second bag activate. I really, really hadn't thought this through!

The explosion blasted, pushing me back into the last machine with such force that I finally came loose from the metal, but not without a gash on my leg. I slammed back against the conveyor belt, and a shot of pain traveled up my spine, immediately giving me a thudding headache.

But I couldn't stop. I was so close. People were running around like they didn't know what to do. Some were helping others up, while others trampled whoever was in their way. I had to move, and quickly. The last bag would explode soon, and I was standing right next to it.

Without thinking, I pulled myself together and continued running toward the stairway. Well, limping was more of an accurate description. Searing pain shot through my leg with every step I took, but I forced myself to move faster. I pushed through the Tainted blocking my way. At that moment, they didn't regard me as their enemy. I don't even think they actually saw me. They were more concerned about their own survival than anything their boss wanted.

So much for loyalty.

I'd just made it to the base of the metal stairway when I saw the last bag starting to light up.

Shit. Shit. SHIT! Move, move, move!

I willed myself to move faster. To climb faster. To make it to the top before the explosion. But the faster I tried to move, the slower I seemed to go. It felt as if the stairs kept extending and lengthening.

I had just stepped onto the platform at the top of the steps when the hex bag exploded. I shielded my face with my arms from the heat of the explosion. The force felt like a heated punch in the gut that propelled me backwards through the double doors, knocking the wind right out of me.

I landed hard on my back, gasping for air. White stars danced across my vision, a high-pitched ringing piercing my ears. Gasping, grabbing at air that kept evading me, pain slammed through my entire body. I couldn't even pinpoint what hurt the most.

Everything was blurred as my vision returned to me. I was seeing double, and I hoped I didn't have a concussion. Through the ringing in my ears, I could have sworn I heard voices. But then again, the factory was buzzing with so much noise that anything was possible.

A shadow drifted above my vision. I struggled to make it out. The person was talking but I couldn't understand a word they were saying. I tried to focus on the image, to make my eyes work as they were supposed to, but to no avail.

The shadow inched closer. My vision still danced, the double images jumping around, but at least the darkened edges had started receding a bit. A powerful grip tugged at my face as I tried sitting up, but the pain was excruciating.

This was not good.

The shadow came into view as he gripped my face harder, adding to the already painful list of my body. Dakin's eyes looked at me, only it wasn't Dakin. The amber hue shone in the blue of his eye.

I was face to face with Gorice again, but this time on his territory. I looked at him, still not hearing a word he was saying, then suddenly his fist connected with my jaw, sending me into the darkness of sleep.

CHAPTER 27

My body seemed to consist only of a pounding ache as I started to wake. I couldn't place what hurt more—my body or my head. Out of habit, I wanted to touch my head, but my arms were restrained. My eyes shot open as I remembered what had happened. A ceiling fan stained yellow from age wobbled as it spun overhead.

Gingerly, I looked around and found myself in one of the offices. Two large tables stood opposite each other. The door had been blown off its hinges and lay on the floor, accompanied by shattered glass and strewn papers. I tried to sit up again, but when the restraints restricted me from doing so, I noticed I was tied on a third table.

"Well, that's just great."

"So, my soul has finally awoken. Marvelous." A figure stepped out from behind me, and I had to strain my neck to see Gorice still prancing around in Dakin's body. My knee-jerk reaction was to jump off the table and beat the living shit out of him, but the restraints held me tight.

"So feisty and tenacious. I love it. Too bad you won't be for long." Gorice laughed as he walked around me like a predator watching his prey.

Unfortunately for him, I was not that sad, little damsel I'd been when I was first attacked.

"Let me go and I'll show you feisty." I pulled at the straps, hoping it would give way, but it didn't.

"Ooh, such vehemence. I could have used you in my army. You have so much spirit."

"I'll never join your Tainted trash," I spat.

Gorice's face twisted with anger, but he quickly composed himself. "Tainted. Such a degrading word. Let me guess who came up with that . . . my brother?"

"Leave Ryker out of this!"

"If I wanted him here, I wouldn't have put him in the coma, would I?" He leaned over me with a smug look on his face.

"You son of a bitch!" I screamed, tugging at the straps as hard as I could, and my arm came loose. Without thinking, I swung and punched Gorice in the face. He staggered back a few steps, rubbing his jaw. It felt good to have landed one, but before I could try to release myself, the Tainted in the room came up to me to hold me down. I swung my arm wildly, knocking an elbow against a stomach and when another came to hold my shoulders in place, I sat upright and headbutted the guy.

I wasn't going down without a fight.

"Let me go!" I screamed as more Tainted came to hold me down.

"Now, why would I want to do a thing like that?" Gorice asked. "I have so many plans for you. Or rather, for your soul."

"Go fuck yourself. I'm not giving you shit."

"Language! Do you kiss your mother with that mouth?" He smirked at me.

I glared at him. I couldn't wait to kick the living shit out of him. There were a lot of scores to settle, and I would be the one to do it. Kaye, my mother, Ryker, Dakin. Those were just the ones that I was aware of. I pulled against the Tainted's hands, but they'd tied me to the table again.

Great.

When they were done, most of the idiots left the room, with only a few of them remaining. Probably to protect their amazing leader that was so powerful he had to possess a teenage boy. I mentally rolled my eyes at the stupidity.

"I am not giving you my soul."

"Didn't we already have this conversation? If you don't give me your soul, I will have to persuade you." He grabbed one of the chairs and sat close to me, keeping his distance just in case I decided to do anything else. "Oh, and don't even try using your powers. We have warded the table you're tied to. A protective measure."

"You're so thoughtful. Not," I retorted, trying to sound bored. I was screwed. I had no way to fight back. "I'm still not giving you anything."

"Do you really want me to hurt your . . . what do the kids call it these days? BFF?"

"No, but the good of the world outweighs that of my own heart." I blinked back tears and stared at the wobbling fan above me.

"I see you've become acquainted with Kaye. How is she lately? Still a pain in the ass as always?"

I didn't like the look on his face. He contorted Dakin's smile into something so sinister that my best friend had lost all his goofiness. I couldn't stand it. Gorice waited for me to reply, but I kept my mouth shut.

"Oh, come now. We were having so much fun getting to know each other."

"Just get it over with."

"You see, that is where we have a bit of a problem." He stood and started pacing around the table. I became dizzy as I followed his movements. "If I try to take your soul forcefully, it would just cross over into the ethereal and then into the afterlife with your darling mother and grandmother." He spat the words out as if it left a bitter taste in his mouth.

"I need you to give me your soul willingly. That way I can have the power of the last Pure."

"And what would you do with that power? Take over the world? So cliché."

"Some would call it world dominance, but I find that term to be quite . . . limited." He whispered the last word in my ear as he passed by, giving me goosebumps. "No. To have so many people in power, with power, it all just seems to have divided the world even more."

"So what? You want to unite us all? What a saint."

"See, even you get that. I sure am going to miss that smart mouth of yours, but it's either your sass or your soul, and I think you know which one I prefer."

"Okay, so you want to get rid of all the people who have power and are in power.. What about your minions? Do they get to decide?" I challenged. I needed him distracted while I tried to figure a way out of this. My backpack was somewhere in this room, but it was of no help now. I didn't have any rings on me, nor did I have anything in my pockets. The only thing I had was—

"My people have been loyal to me for hundreds of years. Once I have your soul, I can conjure back my body and my powers. I will be unstoppable. Besides, my Tainted, as you so aggressively call them, would hand me their power without hesitation."

"You mean with fear. That's the only thing that's keeping them loyal to you. Fear."

"Fear. Loyalty. Aggressive persuasion. Call it what you wish. It's all the same. At least I have someone here with me. Where are your 'people?'" He mocked me with air quotes.

I knew he was talking about Mae and the coven. He laughed as he grabbed his chair and spun it around, sitting on it in reverse style. The two Tainted in the room paid no attention to him. It was as if they were all brainwashed.

"So, what's it going to be? You know I am a very patient person, Amunet. I've waited for you for so long. What's a couple of decades strapped to a desk?"

My silence served as my answer.

"Maybe I can coax you over to my side?"

"Never."

"Well, then, I guess I better get creative." He stood and moved to my legs.

With no warning, a searing pain burned up my leg. I screamed. Gorice pressed harder on the gash I had on my leg from where the metal had hooked me earlier. The pain intensified with the pressure, and I screamed so loud and long that I went hoarse. He let go and moved to my side. Tears fell unbidden from my eyes at the agonizing pain. The wound throbbed, almost as if my heart was beating in my leg instead of my chest.

"Just say the words and it will all be over."

"Never," I croaked, feeling the burn in my throat.

A blow landed on my ribs, and I heard it crack. The howl inside me stuck to my throat as another blow knocked the wind out of me. I gasped for air when Gorice landed another blow. Every breath was a struggle.

Pain roared through me as my body spasmed, trying to shy away from the blows, but I couldn't. I couldn't move. I couldn't do anything.

I wouldn't be making it out of here.

A knock at the entrance drew Gorice's attention from me, and I whimpered in relief.

"What is it?" he shouted through clenched teeth. One of the Tainted stood there, not sure what to make of the scene in front of her.

"There's . . . Someone's here and wants to see you. Says he's your brother."

Gorice's face looked as if someone had thrown him with ice water.

CHAPTER 28

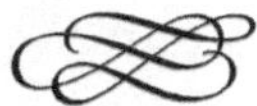

Gorice composed himself, then left me gasping for air on the table. Every breath I took hurt. I felt hopeless and useless. I couldn't even come up with a plan to get myself out of this situation and even if I could, I didn't think I would have the strength to go through with the plan.

Shouts reverberated through the factory from below. I couldn't make out what was said, but it was a definite screaming match. Neither of them was very friendly right now. After a few minutes, the shouting died down to a more passionate argument. The voices were still raised, but not as loud as they had been before.

It was silent for a while, and my breathing returned to a semi-normal state, though still rapid. Not too long after, I heard footsteps on the metal staircase leading up to the top office. My heart raced as the steps got louder. I didn't want to see Gorice come back only to beat the crap out of me some more, so I closed my eyes and waited for the blows.

"Gorice, you son of a bitch!" a familiar voice sounded through the room as a soft, caressing hand stroked my hair and my face.

My eyes flicked open, and I cried out from happiness.

"Ryker?" I choked out, my throat thick with emotion. He was a welcoming sight, even in his battered and bruised body.

"Shh, I'm here, honey. I'm here." He soothed me with his gentle touch as his eyes roamed my face and then moved toward the rest of me. "Goddess, Gorice. What have you done? Is this really necessary?" Ryker stood and gestured to me strapped to the table.

"Yes. She took out more than half of my men. She's much stronger and capable than you think, brother."

"You haven't been my brother in a long time." Ryker turned to me, still touching me. I didn't know if he was trying to convey a message to me or just trying to console me.

"Now, brother, that is not a gracious thing to say. Especially since I will be hosting your granddaughter's soul soon."

"Over my dead body!" Ryker jumped into a fighting stance.

"That can be arranged," Gorice said as he motioned to his Tainted followers to attack Ryker. Even in his weakened state, Ryker managed to use his powers to knock two of the Tainted against the walls, but I could see it drained him faster than usual.

His knees buckled, and he sank to the ground, breathing hard. I knew that feeling, and I could see in his face that he wanted to fight, to carry on fighting, but his body just didn't want to cooperate.

Gorice strode leisurely toward Ryker and landed a punch squarely in his face.

I didn't care about the asshole standing in front of me. All I wanted was to make sure Ryker was okay.

"Now, my dear, are we going to do this the hard way or the easy way? I have so much unfinished business with my brother. I wouldn't mind some *bonding* time with him." The way he said the word bonding sent chills down my spine.

"Amunet, don't—" Ryker didn't have time to finish as Gorice turned around and kicked Ryker in the chest, sending him rolling on the ground.

"No! Don't! Stop it! Please, just stop it!" I begged as I struggled on the desk. The straps cut into my flesh as I tried to loosen them. Nothing helped. Ryker rolled, coughing, but managed to speak.

"This will never work. You can't bring her back."

"What did you say?" Gorice stopped in his tracks and turned around again, facing Ryker.

"You can't bring Kaye back. No matter how much power you possess." Ryker started sitting up, wincing as he moved. "Kaye would never allow it. You turned. Became Tainted. She will never love you. Not what you have become." That sent Gorice into a fit of rage.

He stormed to Ryker, grabbing him by the shirt and pulling him up as he started pounding on him, shot after shot, screaming as he did so.

"You know nothing of my feelings for her!" he yelled as he kept hitting Ryker.

Fear crept in, clutching at my heart. He would not survive this if Gorice kept at it. I could see Ryker stop struggling against the hold as his arms went limp, but the beating continued.

"Stop it, please, stop it! I'll do it!" I shouted as loud as I could. I just wanted Gorice to stop. "You're killing him, stop it! I'll do what you want." Tears streamed down my face as I fought against my emotions, my fear. I couldn't just lie there and watch Gorice kill the only family I had left. It was too much to handle.

"What did you say?" Gorice stopped mid-swing and turned to me.

"I said I'll do it. Just leave Ryker alone. Please." Gorice smiled as he tossed Ryker to the floor. For a moment, I thought he was dead—there was so much blood—but movement caught my eye as Gorice came to stand in front of me.

"I'm so very pleased to hear that. If I had known he would be your breaking point, I would have used him sooner."

I hated the smug expression on his face. It made the bile in my stomach rise, and I wanted to throw up. Gorice worked on the straps holding me in place and loosened them.

"Let's get you out of this and off the table. Can't really do a spell when your magic is bound. And no funny business. Or my brother dies." He nodded to one of the Tainted still in the room and she made her way to Ryker, her gun pointed at his head, ready to use it as per Gorice's instructions.

He released me from the bonds and pulled on my arm until I was sitting upright. The pain in my side made me wince. I had almost forgotten about the broken ribs he had inflicted on me mere moments ago. I was too tired to focus, but I knew I needed to get through this otherwise people—my family—would die, and I didn't want to be the cause of that. I wouldn't be able to forgive myself for it.

"Don't—" Ryker's ragged voice was barely a whisper, and it made me tear up again. I didn't want to do it, but I had to. I had no choice. As I slid off the desk, my knees gave in, and I fell to the floor.

I was far too weak, and the spell Gorice wanted me to do would be the end of me.

I didn't want to die. I had so much life I still wanted to live. So many things I still wanted to do that I would never be able to do after this moment.

"Come now. I don't have all day." Gorice pulled me to my feet again, this time holding me upright. "Let's go outside. I want the entirety of my people to witness the greatness I will become."

He started leading me toward the door but stopped short.

"What are you doing? Stop this." Gorice shook me.

I didn't know what he was talking about. "I'm not doing anything."

"Don't play coy with me," he seethed, gripping my shoulders, the amber hue in his eyes now burning a reddish color.

"It's not me . . ." I began. But if it wasn't me, the only other person in this room who had this kind of power was Ryker. Turning my head, I stared past Gorice. Ryker was sitting upright with his arm extended.

Gorice turned, following my gaze, and his eyes widened.

"You! Stop this madness now!" Gorice screamed at his brother, but Ryker paid him no attention. His eyes met mine, and it felt like time had stood still.

"I'm sorry," Ryker whispered, staring at me. Then his gaze went to Gorice as he started muttering a spell.

"What are you doing? What's happening?" Gorice complained,

releasing me from his hold. He stared at his brother, who was still muttering the spell, making movements with his hands toward Gorice and toward himself. Back and forth the motions went, faster as the words became louder.

"No, no, no! This is not how it should be!" Gorice yelled.

Footsteps rushed toward us from the walkway, but I was too engrossed in what was happening in front of me to acknowledge the newcomers.

Then, I saw it. Gorice's soul was pulled out of Dakin and suspended in midair for a moment, looking shocked and fearful as it drifted toward —no, this couldn't be happening! Gorice's soul drifted toward Ryker. Glowing a putrid green, it moved and settled into Ryker's body.

Everything was silent. No one moved, no one said a word. Ryker opened his eyes, and I could still see the wonderful man that I had thought to be my uncle in them. I felt relieved. I rushed toward him, but he held up his hand to me, making me stop mid-step.

"Ryker?" I asked, concern etching its way into me. Something was wrong.

"I'm sorry, Amunet. I had to. I love you," Ryker replied, tears shining in his eyes.

He never cried. I wanted to go to him, but my step came up short when a light radiated from Ryker.

At first it was just a small light, but it grew bigger and brighter with every second. I knew what he had done. He had done what Kaye did when she sacrificed herself to save the world.

"No, Ryker, please no!" I cried as the light became so bright that I had to shield my eyes. It was overpowering. Blinding. It shone throughout the entire factory, and everyone took cover, but before we could fear the backlash of the spell, it was over. The light receded into nothing. There was no explosion, no bang. Nothing.

When my eyes adjusted to my surroundings, my heart fell into the darkest pit of despair.

Ryker was gone.

CHAPTER 29

*H*e was gone. There was no one in sight. The space he'd occupied a few moments ago was empty, and only the shape of him remained. This couldn't be happening. How could this be? I ran to the spot and fell to my knees.

Footsteps sounded behind me as the Tainted all moved into the room, probably wondering what had happened and where their leader was. I could hear their arguments of fear. Someone even suggested that I would know what had happened, while another, a woman, relayed what had happened.

I felt . . . empty. The last person in my family had now been taken from me. I had no one left. It all felt like too much. The anger, the hatred. Grief. Despair. Everything hit me all at once, and I couldn't breathe. I was shaking, but no tears fell. Or maybe they did. I didn't know what was happening. I could feel the thread of magic within me warming up my body, coiling through every inch of my being.

"Fuck, she's going nuke."

Someone screamed from behind me, but I didn't care. I heard them run, screaming and shouting, as I let my emotions take over. Increasing my power, using it to build. It consumed me, and I let it. I welcomed the hum of magic. As I released it into the world, I screamed.

The entire factory shook, and the panic from the Tainted fueled the fire already coursing through me. The light within me expanded and exploded, and all I could see was dark.

~

*S*ilence. The sound of my heart breaking. Tears fell freely on the spot Ryker had once occupied. I called upon death, wishing it would take me, too, but it never came. My heart was hollow and numb. *I* felt numb. There was absolutely nothing left of me. How was I to carry on knowing he was gone?

A gentle hand shook me. If it was one of the Tainted, I welcomed their final relief, but nothing came. Not a shot, a stab, nothing.

"Amy?" the voice sounded familiar, like I'd known it all my life but I couldn't place it. "Amy, please," the voice said again, sounding sincere and worried. My eyes drifted open, and right there, hovering above me, was my friend. My familiar. My Dakin.

Relief washed through me as I saw the concern in his blue eyes and the small smile that made Dakin, well, Dakin. I wanted to cry all over again. I sat upright and threw my arms around his neck, squeezing him as hard as I could. This time the tears falling freely were tears of joy.

"It's okay. It's okay. I'm here," Dakin kept whispering to me as he stroked my back. "Come, let's get out of here."

Before I could even try to stand, Dakin placed his arms under my legs and lifted me off the ground. He carried me through the room, down the stairs and through the factory without even breaking a sweat. I held onto him as tight as I could, taking in his scent of vanilla and pine that let me know he was really my Dakin.

The sun beat down in the afternoon light.

How long had I been under Gorice's torture? A day? Two? I came in here at noon, and now it was roughly the same time. What had I missed?

What had happened out here in the world while mine was being ripped apart? Would it ever feel the same again?

"What happened? Where's Ryker?" a woman's voice asked, but I was just too tired to turn my head. No one said a word, but I could feel Dakin shaking his head.

The woman gave a sharp intake of breath. "Oh, Amy . . ." her words trailed off. "Come, let me take you to a safe place."

We were moving again. I heard car doors opening and then closing. Dakin held me tight, never letting me go, just like he'd promised. The vehicle started to move, and the soft rocking of the car ride lulled me to sleep.

I woke a while later, tucked into a warm, soft bed. The blankets gave comfort when my heart broke again as it all came back to me.

Why? Why did all of this have to happen? Why did I have to be the last Pure? My emotions were all over the place, but this time my magic didn't harness it. It was just there. Dormant.

"I was aware of it all, Mae. It was horrible. You didn't see how it broke her."

"I can imagine. I–I just wished she'd trusted me enough to let me in. To let me help her."

"She was trying to keep you safe, to protect you by keeping you out of it. Gorice . . . that's a different kind of darkness. One I hope never to experience ever again."

Mae's and Dakin's voices drifted through the paper-thin walls. I wanted to crawl further into the bed and sleep, but I couldn't bring myself to drift away. I'd been crying and sleeping for who knew how long. I didn't think it had been more than a few hours—Mae wouldn't have left me to wallow that long without something to eat and drink, even if I didn't want anything.

The more I listened to Dakin's retelling of events through the walls, the more the anger overtook my sorrow. It fueled me more, made me want to get up and do *something*. I heard a door open somewhere in the house, then Mae's mother spoke softly.

"It is time. Is she awake?" I couldn't hear any of the responses as the bedroom door creaked open. I closed my eyes and pretended to be asleep. I wasn't ready to deal with people. All the questions and the looks . . . No, I didn't want to go through that yet. A weight settled on the bed, and I felt a hand stroking me slightly.

"I know you're awake. I'm so sorry about Ryker. He was . . . well, he was the best of us. We're holding a memorial for him outside, and I think it would be good for you to join us," Maeveen whispered gently to me. Tears fell down my face, and I tried not to move. She got up and left, closing the door behind her. In the distance, I heard her telling Dakin and Mae I'd join when I was ready.

Tears streamed down my cheeks as I stared up at the ceiling. I heard music playing and chants being sung. My curiosity got the better of me and before I could stop myself, I was halfway down the road toward the enormous bonfire on the beach. Trapped in a daze, I watched the coven dance and move around the fire, singing and chanting in various languages as things were thrown into the fire, letting off sparks of various colors.

"Beautiful, isn't it? Something else to behold."

I jumped at Maeveen's voice behind me. "It is. What is this?"

"We are a diverse group in this coven. Each has their own way of honoring those who have fallen. As the Priestess, instead of forcing only one belief upon them, I encourage them to be themselves. To openly share their heritage with us so we can all learn, grow, and accept."

"Thank you." It was all I could say as I watched everyone honor the life that had been taken from us too soon.

"What will you do now?" Maeveen asked as she stroked my back.

"First, I will honor Ryker. I will grieve and I will heal."

"And then?"

"Then, I will hunt down every last Tainted, and I will make them all pay."

UNTITLED

The End.

To be continued in Book 2 of the Descendants Series—Unveiled.

Follow for updated news:

UNVEILED (ROUGH DRAFT)

It has been two weeks since Ryker died. Two weeks of silence in the house. Of not knowing what to do or whether or not to carry on with life as normal. Don't even think life would ever be able to get back to normal.

What was normal anyway? A year ago, normal would be hanging out with friends, drinking up a storm at Newt's cafe coffee and juice joint that was usually the hotspot for all the young people in town, and just having fun like teenagers were suppose to.

Now... Normal for me consisted of tracking down the Tainted, finding out what happened to Ryker and getting some damn answers for all my questions. None of these were on my to-do list a few weeks ago.

Then again, a few weeks ago, I didn't even know about any of this. I didn't know magic existed or that witches and familiars were real. I didn't even know that I was a descendant of the most powerful magical race known as the Pure.

The Pure were said to be the souls gifted by the gods to maintain the balance of life. They were the people who were suppose to use their magic and power to keep everything in working order and not let the world tumble into darkness. Well, that didn't last long. Gorice, the leader of the Tainted thought that it would be a great idea to get rid of all the Pure, take their powers for himself so that he can rule the world as he see fits. I know, evil villain with a world domination complex is so cliche, at least that's what I thought until I came face to face with him. Now, I didn't know what to think anymore.

It was Gorice's fault that my uncle, who I found out was actually my grandfather, died. He gave his life to save mine and now I feel that it is my duty to rid the world of all the unbalanced Tainted out there before they found a way to resurrect their leader again. This time they won't be coming after me, I will be going after them.

A knock sounded at the front door but I chose to ignore it. I had too much to do and was not in the mood for anyone. I wanted to find the answers that I needed. That my soul craved so that I can get retribution for Ryker. For Kaye. For my mother. There was also one other thing that I needed answers on, but wasn't ready to admit it to myself quite yet.

"Amy! I know you are there!" Mae's voice sounded from the door as she knocked again, this time harder. The more I tried to ignore it, the louder the banging became and then suddenly stopped. I let out a sigh of relief as I was not in the mood for her right now.

Hunching over all the papers and books around me, I heard the soft click of the lock on the front door. Exasperated, I dropped the book on my lap to the floor and made my way to the entryway. There, standing sheepishly in front of me were my two friends, Mae and Dakin. Mae was a witch of the local coven while Dakin was suppose to be my familiar, but right now they were invaders of my space.

"What do you want?" I asked placing a hand on my hip out of annoyance.

"We just came by to see how you are-" Dakin's words dropped as his eyes bulged the size of small saucers.

"What is the name of the goddess have you been doing?" Mae chimed in when it was obvious Dakin wouldn't finish his sentence.

"Research." Looking around now, I could see what had them so horrified. Books and papers were strewn all across the room.

"Oh honey, it looks like a library threw up in here." Mae walked past me into the living room where I was busy working on my 'research'. She turned around the room, scanning every inch of the place before turning back to me. "And what is that awful smell?"

"I don't invade your space and insult your process, now do I?" I crossed my arms over my chest suddenly feeling very self conscious about myself. I was in no mood to be lectured by my friends right now. I had work to do. I had to find the Tainted, find what exactly happened to Ryker. He couldn't just have disappeared without any trace. I hadn't been able to find him in the ethereal either, but that magic was out of my hands right now. Hence all the books in the surroundings.

"Touchy. I'm all for the creative process and for dealing with things in your own way, but this is ridiculous!" Mae's hands gestured to the room. I know it looked bad, but I knew where everything was and it kept me busy and my mind off of losing the only family that I knew.

"What are you even working on?" Dakin asked as he scanned the books laying open on the floor. He bent down and picked one up, checking out the cover and its contents. Mae followed suit and picked up her own book to investigate. With every book they took, they shared a glance with each other and then stared at me.

"I think it's time you tell us what's going on here." Mae suggested as she held up a book showing the cover to me. The golden glint of the title shone in the dim lighting of the room. *How to find your power.*

"I'm too uncaffeinated for this conversation." I muttered and stalked past them towards the kitchen. Without a beat, Mae and Dakin followed me and gasped at the sight. Plates and mugs were scattered around the kitchen table. Pizza boxes littered the small island in the middle of the room while the trash can at the door bubbled over with even more fast food boxes.

"What in the world?" Mae started but I could see her train of thought ran away with her as she looked at the mess.

"I've been meaning to clean up... I was just busy."

"It looks more like you had a frat party in here." Dakin retorted but stifled a laugh as Mae shot him a glare.

"Honey, when was the last time you ate something decent?"

"What day is it?"

"Sit, I'll make you something proper." Mae ordered as she made her way to the fridge. She hardly opened the door then slammed it shut. "Maybe we should go out to eat." She suggested and I knew that the fridge was as empty as a school hall in summer.

"I'm not ready."

"Well why don't you go finish up and Dakin and I will sort this out." Mae suggested as she gave me a sideways hug. "Maybe you should take a shower too. You will feel much better."

"Am I really that bad?"

"Let's just say that the kitchen looks better." Mae shooed me away towards the bathroom and turned towards Dakin.

"Why do I have to clean?" Dakin complained and I could see the mischief in his eyes shining bright.

"Because you are our friend and that's what friends do." Mae mothered as she threw a dishcloth at Dakin, waiting for him to start cleaning.

"Yes mother." He mocked as he scooted off the chair and away from the backhand Mae was getting ready to give him. As I walked away, I could hear her barking orders at Dakin but their voices became muffled as I strode through the darkened hallway towards my bedroom.

The shower did me great and I felt more like myself than I had in days, but the silence of the house lingered like a ghost in the walls reminding me of what use to be. What once was. The urge to run downstairs and dive into the books again felt too strong to ignore, but I knew that if Mae or Dakin see me, they would drag me out of the house as fast as they could. I wanted to continue searching. It kept my mind occupied and my heart from breaking.

That first night back in the house nearly killed me. The emptiness of the rooms echoed my own and at first, I cried. I cried and I screamed. I fought with no one there. I broke. I basically shattered deep within and the only solace I found were the same ones that Ryker use to. His books.

"How's it going up there?" Mae shouted from the stairs and I knew as well as I knew my own name that if I didn't get up and out, she would storm in here and pull me out of the room whether I wanted it or not.

Poking my head through the open door into the hallway I shouted back to Mae. "Almost done. Give me five minutes."

I could just imagine Mae nodded as she walked away with a dishcloth in her hand, probably telling Dakin to finish up in the house or take the trash out. I was fully dressed and ready to go, but I needed some time to place my mask on. The mask that let's people think you are okay and that you are dealing with things very well. The mask that let's people stop asking questions and leave you alone. I hoped that it would work on my friends but they knew me too well and had a tendency to see through all my bullshit, but I had to try.

Mae was waiting for me by the front door, "Now don't you look like yourself again? Dakin's waiting in the truck." She led me outside and it took a while for my eyes to adjust to the brightness of the mid-morning light.

Walking towards the truck, I caught my reflection in the window. I might look like my pre-magical self but I hadn't felt less like me in a long time. It felt like something was wrong with me on the inside and I just couldn't place my finger on what that might be.

ABOUT THE AUTHOR

Lea Cherry is an international bestselling author residing in South Africa with her husband and two daughters. With a Bachelor's degree in Creative Writing, she shares the spark of language in Young Adult, Fantasy, Horror, and Thriller. When she is not crafting stories, she shares her time with her family watching movies, painting, and reading up a storm when she is not exploring the outdoors on camping trips. Her first book in the Descendant series is set to arrive in 2021 and is filled with magic and adventure that will keep you wanting more.

For all sites, find her here:

beacons.ai/leacherry

facebook.com/authorleacherry

twitter.com/lala_lea

instagram.com/leacherryauthor

amazon.com/Lea-Cherry/e/B00BBJICHC%3Fref=dbs_a_mng_rwt_scns_share

bookbub.com/authors/lea-cherry

ACKNOWLEDGMENTS

~

Writing a book is harder than most people would think and if you do not
have a great support system, then you might not be able to find your way.
For this reason I would like to thank the Lord, for giving me the gift of
words so that I can share it with everyone around me and hopefully inspire
others to follow their dreams.
I want to thank Cindy and Leandri who always checked up on me, made
sure I was writing and helped me with ideas when I got stuck. You girls are
awesome!
My hubby, Ben, even though you are not a reader at all, you listened to

my babbling about the books, the ideas and questioned things about being
an author which made it feel that this step in my life was worth it.

To my girls, Eliska and Peyton, you might not be aware of this now, but I
am doing this all for you. Both of you have given me interesting ideas and
concepts which will most definitely be included in many books to come.

To my editor Monique, from The Editrix, thank you for making this
book so beautiful. I couldn't have done it with you. You helped me get rid of
all my South Africanisms and helped a second language English speaker
work out the kinks on my grammar.

To all my family and friends who are interested in my writing and kept
asking the questions about my books, thank you for showing that you care.

Lastly, and most definitely not the least, to you, the reader. Without
people like you, we us authors won't be able to do what we love and entertain
you with our tall tales of lives and worlds that we create. Every share,
review, comment recommendation you make, brings us all closer together
and helps us as authors keep our dreams alive. You are awesome!